ELLIE MAKES HER MOVE

Marilyn Kaye

HOLIDAY HOUSE • NEW YORK

Library of Congress Cataloging-in-Publication Data

Names: Kaye, Marilyn, author.
Title: Ellie makes her move / by Marilyn Kaye.
Description: First edition. | New York : Holiday House, [2021]
Series: The spyglass sisterhood ; #1 | Audience: Ages 8–12.
Audience: Grades 4–6. | Summary: "Twelve-year-old Ellie moves
to a new town, makes unexpected friends, and discovers a
magical spyglass"—Provided by publisher.
Identifiers: LCCN 2019045472 | ISBN 9780823446094 (hardcover)
Subjects: CYAC: Magic—Fiction. | Telescopes—Fiction. | Friendship—
Fiction. | Moving, Household—Fiction.
Classification: LCC PZ7.K2127 Spy 2021 | DDC [Fic]—dc23
LC record available at https://lccn.loc.gov/2019045472

ISBN: 978-0-8234-4609-4 (hardcover)

For Alice Clerc, with love, from her Tatie

one

WHENEVER I START READING A NEW BOOK, I want to know right away who's telling the story. I want to know who the main character is, and how old they are, and if the story is happening now or a long time ago. Or in the future, if it's some kind of science fiction. So before I begin telling my story, I'm going to introduce myself.

My name is Elizabeth Marks, but everyone calls me Ellie. I'm twelve years old, and the strange tale I'm about to tell you is all happening right now, in the middle of January, in a town called Lakeside.

You should probably know that none of this could have happened to a more average person. I'm all *about* average. Average height, average weight, brown hair, brown eyes. Light skin, a few freckles. Not beautiful, but okay-looking. I usually do pretty well at school, but I'm not a genius. I'm fine at sports, but I'll never be a superstar athlete. I've taken piano lessons and ballet lessons, but I'm not going to be a concert pianist or prima ballerina. I don't have any real talents.

I'm ordinary. Absolutely, positively ordinary. And a few months ago, I was an ordinary, happy seventh grader at Brookdale Middle School on the other side of the state. I'd lived in Brookdale all my life and I had lots of friends. I liked school, and I got along most of the time with my parents and my older sister, Charlotte. When Charlotte went off to college this past September, I got to move into her much-bigger bedroom. All in all, it was a good life.

Then my dad did something that made everyone hate us.

No, he didn't rob a bank or anything like that. He started a massive campaign to raise money to build a homeless shelter in Brookdale. I thought that was a good thing to do, because I knew people were sleeping on the streets in town and that was really sad. My mom supported the idea too, and so did my sister. But it didn't work out so great for us, because it turned out that a lot of people didn't want a homeless shelter in Brookdale. Maybe they thought people without homes were criminals or something stupid like that, I don't know. Anyway, people started writing nasty letters to the newspaper and leaving nasty notes in our mailbox and making nasty phone calls, and pretty soon, it seemed like nobody liked us anymore.

Except for the one nice rich man who was on board with Dad's idea. He jumped in and decided to donate some land and a gazillion dollars or something to build the shelter. People probably hated him too, but he didn't care. He didn't have to. He was like a hundred years old, he owned an island somewhere, and he was hardly ever in Brookdale anyway.

So Dad got the shelter built, but we suffered for it. Dad lost clients. My mom was voted out as president of the PTA. People gave us looks when we went out, and Charlotte didn't want to come home for Thanksgiving so she wouldn't run into her old high school classmates. My parents were fed up with Brookdale and decided to move.

So here we are now, in Lakeside, which already has a homeless shelter so my father can't get into any trouble. And it's been okay for everyone else in my family. Dad was bored with his job at a big corporate law firm and had wanted to start his own business anyway. Good for him. My mom, who used to mostly be at home or out doing volunteer work, was seriously thinking about going back to work full-time. Good for her. Charlotte didn't care about the move because she had left home anyway and was having a great time at college.

But in the middle of seventh grade, just after winter break, on top of everything else, I had to start a new school, East Lakeside Middle. Not so good for me. Now, I don't mean to sound like I think I'm more important than the people who needed that shelter, because I'm not. I'm glad it got built. But personally, in my family, I think I was the one who suffered the most from what happened.

There's one last thing I want to tell you about myself. I've always been a pretty down-to-earth kind of person. I've never believed in ghosts, or zombies, or monsters, or anything like that. I like reading books about magic, but I've never thought it happens in real life.

Here in Lakeside, that was all about to change.

But now I'm getting ahead of myself. It's time to start the story.

◆

On my third day at East Lakeside Middle School, I sat alone in the cafeteria at lunchtime, just as I'd done for the past two days. And I wondered if all the middle schools in the whole wide world were exactly alike. Were they all made of yellow brick? Did they all have the same pukey green walls, the same gray metal lockers, the same boring food? Even some of the teachers here reminded me of teachers back at Brookdale. The science teacher, Mr. Clark, was bald and wore wire-rimmed glasses, just like my old science teacher. My English teacher, Ms. Gonzalez, was young and pretty and smiled a lot, just like Ms. Henson, my favorite teacher at Brookdale.

Looking around the cafeteria, I saw that boys and girls sat separately, just like at Brookdale. There wasn't any rule about that, it's just what they chose to do. And I could spot the same kind of cliques we had at Brookdale. There were the sporty kids, who had short hair or wore running headbands and dressed in T-shirts with the names of basketball teams or sneaker company logos on them. The brains, who all had their heads together and looked like they were very important people discussing something serious. And there were the popular girls, who looked just like the popular girls back home. They wore nice clothes, they had nice hair, and when other kids passed their table, they looked at these girls with admiration and maybe a little jealousy. The girls all seemed very content and sure of themselves.

Back at Brookdale, I was one of them. Yes, I confess: I was a popular girl. Not the *most* popular girl, and certainly not one of the mean ones, but definitely in that clique. Maybe it was just because I looked like them and I'd known them since kindergarten, but I sat at the popular table in the cafeteria and I went to the sleepovers and I generally felt pretty content and sure of myself too.

Then my dad ruined my life. Like I said, people were angry at him, and they passed these feelings on to the whole family. All of a sudden, I started to be excluded—from a birthday party here, a sleepover there, a shopping trip. Friends stopped speaking to me. And one day, there wasn't a seat for me at the cafeteria's popular table.

That hurt. I mean, it really, really hurt. I couldn't believe those girls would act like that. Even Lily, my very best friend. At the beginning, she told me she felt awful about other kids being snotty, and she still came over to my house to do homework together. But then she started making excuses, and she stopped asking me to spend the night like she used to. Finally, she texted that her parents had said she'd be grounded if she hung out with me. And I had a feeling the others in our group told her to quit talking to me or they'd dump her too.

Thinking about all this now, I had that burning feeling behind my eyes, and I knew tears were forming. So I made myself stop thinking about it by continuing to look around the cafeteria.

I saw people who didn't seem to belong to any clique. Loners. We must have had loners back at Brookdale, but to be honest, I never paid much attention to them.

Now I did. Because I had no intention of seeking out friends here at East Lakeside Middle School, not popular kids or kids in any other clique. I'd seen what friends can do to you. So now, I was officially declaring myself a loner too.

I recognized three other loners from my English class. Along the far wall, I saw the girl with braided black hair and brown skin who sat in front of me and who had spent the entire period playing with a tablet under her desk. A few tables away, there was the pale, round-faced girl with long, curly blond hair who looked at the floor when she came into class, and who walked out when the bell rang without having said a word. And at the table just alongside mine was the goth girl.

I don't know much about the whole goth thing—there wasn't a goth crowd back at Brookdale and I hadn't spotted one here either. To be perfectly honest, the only goth type I'd ever seen was a character in a TV series. The girl at the table next to mine looked like her.

She certainly didn't look like anyone else I'd seen in real life, at least, not in middle school. She had long, straight black hair, black makeup around her eyes, and dark red lipstick. Despite all the makeup, I could see that her complexion was a golden tan color. She was wearing a long black skirt with a black T-shirt. Silver skulls dangled from her earlobes.

I tried to recall her name from roll call—Alice? Alison?

I know, I know, I'd just decided to be a loner myself at this school, but it was very boring sitting there with no one to talk to, and I didn't have anything to read. Maybe I was making decisions too fast. And it's not like I'd sworn to be a loner and signed a legal document or anything.

I'm not trying to make a friend, I told myself. *I just want to stop being bored.*

I got up, lifted my tray, and went over to the goth girl's table.

"Okay if I sit here?" I asked.

She looked up and stared at me as if I was

speaking a different language. But she didn't say no, so I sat down across from her.

"I'm Ellie. I'm new here."

No "Pleased to meet you" or anything like that. She turned her attention back to her food.

"We're in the same English class," I said.

She stabbed a carrot with her fork and put it in her mouth. I waited till she finished chewing.

"The teacher seems nice."

Was that a shrug?

"You're...Alice?"

"Alyssa."

She spoke! Okay, so maybe direct questions would work.

"Do you know what we're going to be reading next?" I asked.

Another shrug. She picked up her spoon and started eating the pudding.

So I began to eat my pudding in silence too. But I guess I'm just sociable by nature. I couldn't help myself, I had to talk.

"There's something I was wondering about," I said. "This town, it's called Lakeside. But I haven't seen the lake. Where is it?"

She scraped her spoon around the pudding cup and ate the last bit of it. Then she spoke again.

"There's no lake."

"Then why is it called Lakeside? That doesn't make sense."

She put her spoon down, rose, and picked up her tray. But at least she offered some parting words.

"Nothing here makes sense." With that, she walked away.

I would remember those words later. But at that moment, all I could do was let out a sigh so loud I could actually hear it. And I went back to my pudding.

two

BACK IN BROOKDALE, WE HAD A NICE HOUSE. It was modern, mainly on one floor, but there was a basement that had been turned into a rec room, with paneled walls and a comfortable sofa and a big-screen TV. I had sleepovers down there, and we could make as much noise as we wanted without bothering anyone.

Mom and Dad wanted something completely different in Lakeside, so they bought a house that's more than a hundred years old. It's got two floors, but really three, because there's this weird sort-of round tower on top of the house. I haven't been up there yet because the stairs are falling apart and my parents said it was too dangerous to climb them.

In this old house, the floors creaked, the windows made noise when you opened them, and there was old-fashioned wallpaper everywhere. Mom called it charming. I thought it was creepy, and if I believed in ghosts (which, like I said before, I don't), I'd think it was haunted.

When I came home after school that day, I could hear my mother on her phone in the kitchen.

"That's wonderful, Charlotte, what great news! I'm so pleased." There was a pause. "No, he's in a meeting right now, but I'll tell him when he's finished." Another pause. "All right, darling, we'll talk later. Bye!"

She was hanging up her cell when I came into the kitchen.

"What's so wonderful?" I asked.

"Your sister got into that special film seminar she wanted to take, the one that was already filled. Someone dropped out and she got a place!"

I was not surprised. In my humble opinion, Charlotte always got everything she wanted.

"That's nice," I said, in a way that made it clear I couldn't care less.

Mom ignored my tone. "How was school today?"

"Same as yesterday." I opened the refrigerator door, even though I wasn't hungry.

"There are cookies," my mother said.

I shut the door. "No thanks."

"I've got some news too," she went on. "They called me back for another interview at the *Lakeside County News.*"

When my parents got married, my mother was a reporter. She quit her job when she had kids, but she's always talked about her old career a lot. Now that Charlotte wasn't home much, she'd decided to go back to work, and she was excited about this. I guess she figured I didn't need that much attention anymore.

"That's nice," I said again, with no more enthusiasm than I'd showed the first time I said it.

Mom looked at me in silence for a few seconds. Then she said, "Tell me about school."

"Nothing to tell," I said. "It's just like any other school."

I knew I was being obnoxious, but I couldn't help myself. Then my father came in.

"Hi, kiddo," he greeted me.

"Hi."

Back in Brookdale, when Dad worked at a firm

with a hundred other lawyers, he used to come home late almost every night, and he traveled a lot. When we moved, he announced that he wanted to change his life. He was going to set up his own private practice, in an office right here at home, and work with people who really needed his help.

"How was your meeting?" Mom asked. "Who were those people, anyway?"

"A couple of local bigwigs. They want me to serve as legal consultant for the new town planning committee. They have some really exciting ideas, and it's a great opportunity to get involved."

He looked very happy. My mother looked happy too. And away at school, Charlotte was happy. I knew I should be glad they were all happy. Instead, I opened the refrigerator door again. Nothing had changed since the last time I looked. And I slammed the door shut.

I didn't realize it would make so much noise. Both my parents stared at me.

"Ellie, are you all right?" my father asked.

"Fine," I snapped. "Just fine."

They exchanged looks, and my mother's lips tightened. I knew that expression. I took a step back.

"You know, Ellie, this hasn't been easy for any of us. We're all starting over here."

I said nothing.

Then she took a deep breath and spoke brightly. "The carpenter finished repairing the stairs today. You can go up and see the turret. There's an old telescope in there. Find out if it still works!"

What a thrilling idea, I thought sarcastically, but somehow managed not to say it out loud. I wondered if I could shrug as well as Alyssa-the-goth-girl did. I tried. And then I walked out, climbed one flight of stairs, went into my room, and threw myself on the bed.

I knew I was feeling sorry for myself, and I was acting like a spoiled brat. It was all so wrong, and really not like me at all. But I couldn't help myself. Life was just so unfair sometimes!

I lay there for a moment, staring at the blank walls and the boxes on the floor. I should start unpacking, put some posters on the walls, make this place feel like home. But I wasn't in the mood. On the night table, there was a book I was in the middle of, but I didn't feel like reading now. And I also had some homework. I didn't want to do that either.

So I got up and went down the hall to the stairs that had just been fixed. They were steep and narrow and curved around in a spiral, so I held tight to the rail. At the top, I opened the door and entered the tower thing. The turret, my mother called it.

It was a strange little room, round, with small windows. The floors were bare and there was no furniture. The only thing in it was a telescope, mounted on a stand in front of a window. It looked like the stand was nailed to the floor.

It wasn't ours. It must have belonged to the people who lived here before. Maybe they were bird watchers, or they looked at stars. I walked across the room and examined it more closely.

I had to admit, it was pretty cool. You could tell that it was really old. There was the kind of design on it that you don't see on modern stuff, shapes and swirly things. But for something so old, the brass was still really shiny.

It definitely worked. I looked through it, and I could see half the town. And it swiveled so I could see even more. There was a dial I could turn to zoom in and make things bigger.

We'd driven around a lot, so I recognized some buildings—the library, Town Hall, the medical center. My stupid school. I could see Main Street, with its shops and people moving on the sidewalk. Beyond that, a nice apartment building with a fancy entrance and balconies.

There was one place I hadn't noticed before. It was a big modern building, bright blue and yellow, and I could make out the words LAKESIDE COMMUNITY CENTER over the entrance. And just beside it, there was an outdoor swimming pool. I could even see people splashing around in the sunshine.

"Ellie! Dinner's ready!"

Reluctantly, I stepped back from the telescope. And I shivered. The heating wasn't great in this house, but it was going to be fixed. And very soon, I hoped. It was the middle of winter, for crying out loud.

And that was when I suddenly realized that what I'd just seen through the telescope was crazy and impossible. This was January, too cold for swimming outdoors, even if the pool was heated. Not to mention the fact that it was twilight—there was no sunshine. I shivered harder.

"Ellie!"

Maybe it was just my imagination, I thought as I went downstairs. Summer was my favorite season, and I used to love hanging out at the public pool back in Brookdale. Wishful thinking, that's all it was.

My parents eyed me anxiously as I approached the table, and I tried to put on a more cheerful face. It became easier when I saw dinner.

"Mm, meat loaf," I said. "*And* mac and cheese? All my favorites!" Now I felt really bad for the way I'd been behaving, and I decided to make a real effort.

"Do you think you'll get that job, Mom?" I asked, settling into my chair.

"I hope so. It's a regional newspaper that covers all the towns in this area, so it should be pretty lively. You've seen it, we started having it delivered when we moved here."

I nodded. Then I turned to my father. "So this planning committee you're consulting for—what do they plan?"

"Well, the biggest thing they're working on is the community center..."

"Yeah, it looks nice."

His eyebrows went up. "How do you know that?"

"I saw it." I took a big bite of meat loaf.

"You mean you saw the architect's drawing in the newspaper?" he asked.

"No, I saw the community center," I replied. "From the window upstairs."

My father smiled. "That's not possible, kiddo. It hasn't been built yet. But I appreciate your show of interest."

I swallowed, hard. "Is—is there a swimming pool in Lakeside?"

"Not a public one, no," Dad said. "But there's going to be one outside the new community center."

"Oh. Okay."

I must have looked a little weird. I sure *felt* a little weird. Had I just seen the future through the telescope? My mother reached across the table and took my hand. "Give Lakeside a chance, honey. You'll get involved, you'll make new friends. You really might love it here."

I highly doubted that, but after this conversation, there definitely *was* something that interested me about Lakeside. I was itching to get back upstairs, but I tried not to rush through dinner. The food was too good, and besides, I had to wait for everyone to finish so I could clear the table, my usual job.

"Do you have homework?" Mom asked when she saw that my plate was empty.

I nodded. "Yeah, lots."

"Then why don't you go ahead and get started. We'll clear up and do the dishes."

"Okay, thanks," I said, and I took off. But I didn't go to my room to start homework. I headed back up to the turret.

Night had fallen, but fortunately, there were enough streetlights on in Lakeside that I could still see the town through the telescope. I pointed it in the direction where I'd seen the blue-and-yellow complex with the sparkling swimming pool. But all I saw this time was an old building with broken windows.

Was I looking in the wrong direction? I swiveled the telescope and moved it slowly. I squinted. Then I switched eyes. That made no difference.

I sighed. Maybe I *did* see the architect's drawing in the newspaper, and I'd just imagined it there, in real life. Like Mom said, we had the paper delivered every day.

But I couldn't remember ever actually looking at it.

I looked through the telescope again, one more time. No community center, no pool. But I did see something else.

Alyssa-the-goth-girl.

On a broomstick.

Flying over the town.

three

IT MUST HAVE BEEN A DREAM. THAT WAS what I kept telling myself the next morning. I even mentally lectured my reflection in the mirror as I brushed my teeth.

Ellie Marks, it never happened. You didn't see that community center, and you certainly didn't see Alyssa on a broomstick. It was a dream. It wasn't real because it couldn't *be real.*

Before I left for school, I went back up to the turret and looked through the telescope again. All I saw was Lakeside the way it really was—no community center. And no goth girl on a broomstick. Which made perfectly good sense, because the community center hadn't been built yet, and there is no such thing as a witch.

Only I couldn't really convince myself, because it all happened before I went to bed. Unless *all* of yesterday was a dream, including the meat loaf and the mac and cheese. Or had I suddenly developed some sort of wild and crazy fantasy life?

Whatever was going on, I had to admit, I was now kind of curious about Alyssa. I didn't see her at school until English class, second period. I got there early, but she didn't arrive until the bell was already ringing, so I had no chance to speak to her.

She wasn't wearing the same black skirt and top she'd had on the day before. This time, it was a dress that looked like a long T-shirt that fell below her knees. But it was black, and she wore it with black tights and black boots, so it was the same look. With that long black hair and her black-rimmed eyes, she didn't need a pointy hat to look like a witch.

When the bell stopped ringing, Ms. Gonzalez took attendance. I listened carefully and caught Alyssa's last name: Parker.

Then the teacher rose from behind her desk.

"Good morning, everyone. I've finished grading the book reports you turned in on Friday, and..." She stopped. "Kiara?"

There was no response.

"Kiara Douglas!"

The girl sitting in front of me looked up from her tablet.

"Put that away, right now!" Ms. Gonzalez ordered.

The girl closed her tablet and stuck it into the backpack that was hanging from her chair.

The teacher looked seriously annoyed. "I've told you before, I've told *all* of you, there will be no playing with phones or electronic devices in this class. And Kiara, if I see that again, I'm confiscating it. Is that understood?"

"Yes, Ms. Gonzalez," Kiara said.

"As I was saying, I've graded your book reports. I must admit, I was dismayed to see so many reports on *Of Mice and Men* and *The Old Man and the Sea*. Both are very fine works of literature, of course. But they are also the shortest books on the reading list, and I think some of you may have chosen them for that reason alone."

I almost smiled. My English teacher back home had said exactly the same thing last term. I couldn't understand why people would do that. When I was reading a good book, it wanted it to last as long as possible.

Ms. Gonzalez continued. "Now, because I think we all can benefit from example, I'd like to read aloud from the best book report I received. This report is not just a summary, it's an actual discussion. The report is on *One Hundred Years of Solitude* by Gabriel García Márquez. And by the way, editions of this book usually run over four hundred pages long."

She paused, as if expecting gasps of admiration. But no one looked particularly interested.

"The report was written by Rachel Levin-Lopez."

That bit of information got some response. There was something that sounded like a snort from the back of the room. And there was something that sounded more like a whimper, which came from the girl with long, curly blond hair who I'd noticed sitting alone in the cafeteria yesterday. The blush that spread across her round face told me she must be Rachel Levin-Lopez.

Ms. Gonzalez picked up the paper from her desk and began to read.

"'*One Hundred Years of Solitude* is the story of the Buendía family, who live in the fictional village of Macondo in Colombia, South America.'"

As she went on, I was impressed. I'd never read this book, but Rachel Levin-Lopez made me want to. The story sounded like it had everything—romance, ups and downs, births, deaths, wars, and it covered more than a hundred years.

As Ms. Gonzalez read, I occasionally glanced at Rachel, who was sinking down in her chair.

When she finished reading, Ms. Gonzalez said, "Gabriel García Márquez is considered to be one of the most important writers from Latin America. He won the Nobel Prize for Literature in 1982."

A kid in the back raised his hand.

"Yes, Jim?"

"If he was from Latin America, how come he wrote a book in English?"

"More specifically, Mr. Márquez was from Colombia, and the book was originally written in Spanish," Ms. Gonzalez told him. "It was translated into English. Rachel, do you happen to know the original title?"

Rachel's response was just barely audible. *"Cien años de soledad."*

Ms. Gonzalez looked even more impressed. "Excellent, Rachel."

The girl sank even lower, practically disappearing under her desk.

"Does anyone have another question or comment?" Ms. Gonzalez asked. No one did. I considered raising my hand to compliment Rachel, but I recalled my decision to be a loner, and loners didn't call attention to themselves. But I still wanted her to know how much I liked the report, so as soon as class was over and the bell rang, I leaped up and walked toward her desk. Just as I got there, a couple of boys passed by and one of them spoke to her.

"So are you a cat or a dog?" he asked.

"Maybe she's a gerbil," his friend said.

Rachel was frantically trying to stuff a book into her backpack and dropped it. I couldn't resist, I had to say something.

"What are you talking about?" I asked them.

"Well, she's teacher's pet," the first boy said. "I'm just wondering what kind of pet."

Laughing, the boys walked out of the room.

Rachel's face was beet red as she got up from her desk. I spoke quickly.

"Hi, I just wanted to tell you—" But before I could get another word out, she scurried away.

By now, Alyssa had left the room too, so I couldn't speak to her either. But I caught up with her at lunch.

She was sitting alone again when I emerged from the line with my tray, and this time I went directly to her table. I didn't ask if it was okay—I just sat down. She didn't look any friendlier than she had yesterday, but at least she didn't object.

I tried to start a conversation with a casual question.

"What did you think of that book report?"

She did her usual shrug.

"I thought it was pretty good," I went on. "Have you read that book?"

She shook her head.

I continued. "I didn't have to write a report, because it was assigned before the holiday break and I wasn't here. What did you report on?"

"*Wuthering Heights,* by Emily Brontë."

"I never read it," I confessed. "But I liked *Jane Eyre.*"

"That's by *Charlotte* Brontë."

"I *know*," I said. "I'm just saying, because they're kind of connected. The authors being sisters."

"*Wuthering Heights* is better," Alyssa said. "It's spooky."

Alyssa did look like the kind of person who would appreciate spooky books. I didn't say that, of course.

Actually, I couldn't think of anything else to say— at least, not anything that could lead to the vision of her that I'd had last night in the telescope. So we ate in silence.

Then a girl stopped by the table.

"Alyssa..."

She looked up and she didn't smile. "What?"

The other girl, with light brown hair pulled back in a single braid, seemed a little nervous.

"Um, I'm supposed to pick some stuff up for the folks this afternoon at the dry cleaner's. But I forgot about a meeting I have with the yearbook committee after school. Do you think you could do it?" She began fiddling in her backpack. "I'll give you the receipt."

"I can't," Alyssa said, without any apology or even looking sorry. "I'm doing something."

The girl bit her lip. "Oh. Okay. I guess I can miss one meeting. Well... see you."

Alyssa didn't reply. When the girl was gone, I asked, "Is that your sister?"

"Stepsister," Alyssa said. "Madison. She's in eighth grade."

"Oh." I hesitated. "So, you're busy after school today?"

"No. I just said I was."

She must have seen my puzzled look, because she explained. "Last night I heard Madison say something on the phone to one of her friends, that sometimes she thinks I'm a total witch. She shouldn't talk about me behind my back like that. So I don't want to do her any favors."

I almost choked on a green bean. "She called you a witch?"

She nodded. "Which a lot of people think I am." She cocked her head thoughtfully. "Actually, I think I maybe *could* be a witch."

I spoke carefully. "You mean, like a Wiccan?"

"Nah, I mean the old-fashioned, fairy-tale type. You know, put curses on people. Cast spells, ride on a broomstick."

When I finally managed to swallow the green bean, I spoke.

"Well, if you're free, I was just wondering if, maybe, you'd like to come over to my house this afternoon."

Alyssa frowned. "What for?"

I formulated my words carefully. "Remember yesterday, when you said nothing makes sense here?"

"Yeah. Why?"

I took a deep breath.

"I want to show you something that's making me think this is true."

four

I DIDN'T KNOW IF ALYSSA WOULD ACTUALLY
show up to meet me, but when I left school after the
last class, I spotted her standing by the exit.

"Hi," I said.

She didn't return the greeting, but she fell into
step alongside me as I started walking.

"How was the rest of your day?" I asked.

She shrugged. It would take around ten minutes
to reach my house, so I had to get some kind of conversation going.

"So, you just have the one sister?"

"*Step*sister," she reminded me. I already knew from what she'd said at lunch that she wasn't too crazy about Madison.

"Sometimes I don't get along with my sister either," I told her. "Of course, it's easier now."

"How come?" she asked.

"Because she's not home. She's away at college."

"You're lucky," Alyssa said. "I wish all of mine were away from home."

"You've got more sisters?"

"Siblings. A younger brother. And an older stepbrother."

From her tone, I got the feeling she wasn't crazy about any of them.

"You don't get along with them either?"

She did one of her shrugs. "I pretty much ignore them." She didn't sound like she wanted to pursue the topic. I tried to think of something else to ask her, but she surprised me by actually asking a question.

"How come you moved to Lakeside?"

I wasn't all that sure I wanted to get into the whole story with her, or with anyone for that matter. I didn't know how people would react to it, if they'd think my whole family was weird. Like I said before, I wasn't planning to make any friends here, but I wasn't up for out-and-out rejection either.

But Alyssa was pretty weird herself, so I figured if I was going to let anyone in on what happened back in Brookdale, it might as well be her. So I told her the story. She paid attention too, and my tale of woe didn't seem to shock her at all. Every now and then, she'd look at me and nod, like she understood and was actually interested.

What was really amazing was when I finished the story and got her response. She didn't offer any sympathy for my plight at all. Instead, her lips twitched into something that almost looked like a smile. That was a first.

"Cool," she said.

I wanted to ask her what she meant by that. Did she think what my dad did was cool? Or was it cool that my friends rejected me? But we'd reached my house, and as I turned to go up the walkway, Alyssa froze.

"You live *here*?"

And I saw another expression on her face that I hadn't seen before. Her eyes widened, her mouth was slightly open. She was stunned.

"Yeah. Why?"

"I walk by this house all the time," Alyssa said. "It's so...so..."

She seemed to be at a loss for words. I suggested one.

"Old?"

"Magical," she said. "Like a house in a fairy tale." She pointed to the turret. "I can picture Rapunzel up there, letting her hair down so the prince can climb up to see her."

That remark took me by surprise. She didn't seem like the kind of person who would still be interested in stories like that. On the other hand, like she said, there were witches in fairy tales, so maybe that explained it.

"What's your house like?" I asked.

She made a face. "New."

"New can be nice," I said. "At least the floors don't make creaky noises."

"I like creaky noises," she replied.

We proceeded up the walkway, but before we reached the house the door opened and my mother came out.

"Hi, Mom. This is Alyssa Parker."

One thing I'll say for my mother, my father too—they're pretty open-minded about people. Like I said, there weren't any goth types back at my old school. In fact, I couldn't remember ever seeing any in Brookdale at all. But Mom didn't look the least bit startled or disapproving. She might have just been thrilled that I was making a friend. I made a mental note to tell her later that I barely knew Alyssa and that she wasn't really a friend. I didn't want her getting any crazy ideas that I might be happy here.

"Hi, Alyssa. It's nice to meet you."

Alyssa mumbled something that could have been a "Pleased to meet you."

"I'm off to another interview with the editor in chief," my mother told us. "Wish me luck! Oh, and a welcome-to-the-neighborhood lady came by today and left a cake. Help yourselves to it."

She headed over to the garage, and we went up the stairs.

"What's she interviewing for?" Alyssa asked.

"To be a reporter at some newspaper."

"Cool."

That was the second word of approval I'd received from the glum goth.

Inside the house, Dad passed us. He was on the phone so he just waved as he crossed the entrance hall to his office on the other side.

"My dad," I told Alyssa.

I didn't get a "Cool" this time, but she nodded as if he was okay.

"Want some cake?" I asked.

"You said there was something you wanted to show me."

I was pleased she wanted to get right to it. "Yeah, it's upstairs."

She followed me up the stairs and down the hall. I pointed to doors as we passed them. "My parents' room. That's my room. Bathroom's there. And that's Charlotte's. There are a couple of other rooms, I don't know what they're going to do with them. Probably a guest room. And my mom wants to turn one into a study if she gets this job."

Alyssa didn't look particularly interested, so I picked up the pace until we reached the winding metal staircase. She followed me up and I led her into the turret.

Alyssa drew in her breath sharply. Instead of a "Cool," this time I got a soft "Wow." And she even elaborated.

"This is amazing. It's, like, spooky. You could do really fun stuff up here."

"Like what?"

"I don't know. Have a séance. Talk to spirits and stuff."

I looked at her a little nervously. Like I said, my parents are pretty open-minded, but I didn't think they'd approve of communicating with the dead regularly in the house. Not that I believed in that stuff, of course.

"That's what I wanted to show you," I said, pointing.

"A telescope?" she asked.

"Yeah. It was here when we moved in. It's kind of special."

She crossed the room and examined it.

"It's really old," she said.

"But it still works," I told her. "Look through it."

Alyssa was a little taller than me, so she adjusted the angle and peered through the eyepiece.

I held my breath. What would it reveal to Alyssa? Herself, on a broomstick? The yet-to-be-built community center? Goblins and ogres dancing on rooftops?

"You can practically see the whole town," Alyssa said.

"Anything...unusual?" I pointed to the dial. "That magnifies what you see."

She fiddled with it. And then, "Huh."

"What?" I asked eagerly. I came closer. "What is it?"

"My house." She stepped aside. I took this as an invitation to look at it.

"It's the low brick one, with the wraparound porch."

"It's nice," I said. "Big."

"Boring," she said.

Obviously, she hadn't seen anything weird. While I had control of the telescope, I did a quick scan of the town, and I was disappointed. There was nothing to see.

"That's what you wanted to show me?" Alyssa asked. "The telescope?"

I nodded, feeling more than a little embarrassed.

But Alyssa didn't look too disappointed. "It's cool. I mean, you could spy on people with this. That's what it used to be called, you know. A spyglass."

Spyglass was a more interesting word than *telescope,* I thought. And I appreciated the word because it was how I'd felt yesterday, when I saw her on the broomstick. Like a spy. But now that Alyssa hadn't seen anything, I was thinking again that it might have been my imagination. Or maybe the telescope—the spyglass—would only show strange stuff to me.

"Well. I guess I should go."

I felt like I had to do something to make the trip worthwhile for her. "Want some cake first?"

I got one of her usual shrugs, but I saw her head bob slightly, and I took that as a yes.

Back downstairs, Alyssa paused to look at a framed photo of my family on a table next to the sofa.

"That's your sister?"

"Yeah."

"She's a lot older than you."

"Eighteen." Recalling Alyssa's attitude toward her sister—*step*sister—I felt like I had to add something to show some solidarity by saying something negative about Charlotte. "She can be bossy."

Alyssa nodded knowingly.

I found the cake on the counter in the kitchen. A large slice had already been cut from it.

"Looks like my dad helped himself," I said as I cut two more slices and put them on plates.

"Why is your father home during the day?" Alyssa asked.

"He's a lawyer. He has his office here. Milk?"

She nodded and I poured two glasses.

"And you said your mom's a reporter?"

I handed her the glasses and added forks to the plates. "She will be, if she gets this job," I replied as we set everything on the kitchen table. And as we sat down, I asked, "What about yours?"

"My what?"

"Your family. You know all about mine, now tell me about yours."

She looked a little surprised, almost annoyed, and I half expected her to tell me it was none of my business. Or maybe no one had ever asked her anything personal before.

But then she shrugged and dug her fork into the cake.

"Yeah, I guess that's fair." She took a bite, maybe taking time to consider my request. The cake seemed to give her courage, and she began to speak.

"Okay, here goes. My mom's a heart surgeon who developed some new technique of doing something with catheters and now she's famous."

"Famous?" I asked, hearing the doubt in my voice.

"Don't tell me you've never heard of Gina Khatri, MD, cardiac catheter wizard to the stars," she said sarcastically. She took another large chomp of cake before clarifying. "Not like famous in the whole world, just with other heart surgeons." She stabbed her fork into the cake again. "And my stepfather's a big-shot architect, he's won awards. He's building the new community center here."

"I saw it!" I exclaimed.

She looked at me oddly, and I amended that.

"I mean, I saw his plans. Of what it's going to look like."

She continued. "My stepsister, Madison, the girl you saw in the cafeteria? She's a figure skater, she's won a bunch of competitions, and she wants to go to the Olympics."

"Wow, that's amazing!" That slipped out, and I regretted it immediately. Alyssa glared at me, and for a minute I thought she'd get up and leave. But she must have liked the cake, because she just took a deep breath and another bite before going on.

"My stepbrother, Josh, is a senior at Lakeside High. He's captain of the football team, president of the student body, he's on the honor roll, and he's already been accepted to three Ivy League schools."

I was on the verge of another "Wow" but I managed to hold it back.

"And then there's my younger *real* brother, Ethan. He's only nine and he's already a real actor. He's been in three TV commercials and he's acted in lots of shows at the Lakeside Playhouse."

I couldn't resist any longer. "Wow," I blurted out. "You live in a house full of stars."

"No kidding," she said, but there was no pride in her tone. She actually sounded bitter. "Everyone thinks I must be jealous. But I'm not, because I have my own identity and I'm nothing like any of them."

I nodded. "Because you...you're..." I was about to say "a goth" but she beat me to it.

"A goth."

"What is that, exactly? Is it just the way you dress?"

"No. I'm a socially alienated lost soul who has rejected the mainstream culture."

She rattled that off in a way that made me suspect she'd memorized it from a dictionary definition.

I was curious. "So, what *is* your culture?"

"Huh?"

"Well, you said you reject mainstream culture. So what's the goth culture?"

She stared at me for a few seconds. Then she said, "We don't smile a lot."

I gazed at her skeptically. "There's got to be more to it than that."

She hesitated. "There's—there's music, I think. And video games, maybe."

"What else?"

"What's with the third degree?" She glared at me.

I just looked at her. I wasn't going to let her off the hook so easily.

She rolled her eyes. "Look, I just saw some kids who dressed like this when my family went to New York last summer. Everyone else thought they looked awful—I thought they were cool. And the kids looked like they didn't care what anyone thought about them. So when we got back here, I started wearing the makeup and dressing like them. That's all."

I understood. "How does your family feel about it? How you dress, and the way you don't smile much."

"I don't actually care how they feel about it. But, since you asked, they don't like it." For one second, a grin crossed her face. "Which is another good reason to do it. And like I said, Madison thinks I'm a witch."

I considered her thoughtfully. "Do *you* think you're a witch?"

There was a moment of silence. She seemed to be having a mental debate with herself.

Then she spoke. "Like I said before, I wouldn't mind being a witch and having a few magical powers. But I can't do any of that stuff, like spells and curses. I don't know any magic, I don't fly on broomsticks. But I wish I could do magical stuff. Like make some people disappear."

"Like who? Your family?"

"Not for forever," she said hastily. "I mean, I don't want them dead! Just...just to not *be* there once in a while. When they bug me. And I'd maybe like to curse the mean girls at school. Give them all pimples or something. And...and...make chocolate healthier than vegetables. And make boring teachers more interesting. And be invisible when I want to be!" She sighed. "Yeah, sometimes I wish I could be a witch."

It was the perfect opening. And I just *had* to tell her. I took a deep breath. "Alyssa...When I said I had something to show you that didn't make any sense...it wasn't just the spyglass. It's what I *saw* in the spyglass."

"What did you see?"

"You know the community center? The one your stepfather's going to build? I saw it. Like, it was already there—fully constructed. With an outdoor pool and everything."

I couldn't tell from her face what Alyssa was thinking. Probably that I was completely crazy. But I continued anyway.

"And then I saw...you." I took a deep breath. "On a broomstick. Flying."

She stared at me, with no expression at all on her face. She said nothing. I swallowed, hard. Did she think I was nuts?

Finally, she spoke. "Can we go look through it again?"

We hadn't finished our cake, but that didn't matter. We left the table and ran up the two flights of stairs.

"You go first," Alyssa ordered. "Maybe it only shows the weird stuff to you."

Slowly, I scanned the town, twisting the magnifier dial so I wouldn't miss anything.

"See anything?"

"Not really. But I recognize someone."

"Who?"

"That girl in our English class. The one who wrote the book report Ms. Gonzalez read aloud. She's walking with some lady."

I stepped aside and let Alyssa look.

"Oh, yeah. Rachel." And then she gasped.

"What?" I asked.

"Look!"

I saw the same woman I'd seen a few seconds earlier. And the girl by her side had the same long, curly blond hair. But...

"She's a little kid!" I exclaimed.

"And she's holding the woman's hand, right?" Alyssa asked.

"Yes!"

"Let me see again!" Alyssa begged.

I turned the spyglass over to her.

"She couldn't be more than five for six years old," she said. "I don't get it!" Then she turned to me.

"Now look again."

I did. There was the same woman, now walking with the Rachel I recognized from class.

"What does this mean?" I wondered out loud.

"Not a clue," Alyssa whispered. Then she smiled, a real smile.

"But it's like I told you, right? Nothing here makes sense."

five

THE NEXT DAY BEFORE ENGLISH, THERE WERE still five minutes to go before the bell rang. Alyssa and I sat at adjoining desks in the empty classroom, waiting. We'd raced to get there early in hopes of catching Rachel before class started.

"You know," Alyssa said, watching the door, "when I told you nothing here makes sense, I didn't mean this town was magical or anything. I was just being my socially alienated self."

I nodded. "Yeah. I got that. But I don't think it's Lakeside that's magical," I replied. "It's the spyglass."

She nodded back.

"You know what," I continued, "when I saw the community center, and I found out that it hadn't even been built yet, I thought maybe the spyglass could show me the future. But then that wouldn't explain why I saw you on a broomstick."

Alyssa considered this. "Unless I'm going to turn into a witch someday."

"Do you believe that could happen?"

"No," Alyssa admitted. She turned to look at me. "Maybe the spyglass is showing you fantasies, what people want. Like, according to my stepfather, people in Lakeside have been wanting a community center for a long time."

I nodded. "That makes sense. And you said that sometimes you daydream about being a witch, or having magic powers. But how does that explain what we saw Rachel doing?"

"Maybe she wishes she was a little kid again. I mean, she never looks very happy."

"*You* never look very happy," I pointed out.

"Yeah, but not because I wish I was a child. I'm a lost soul, remember?"

"Oh, yeah, right."

Now it was only two minutes till the bell, so people started drifting into the room. The girl who had the desk next to mine came toward us and looked at Alyssa through narrowed eyes.

"You're in my seat," she said.

Alyssa did her shrug thing. "Bell hasn't rung yet."

"Yeah, well, I just don't want you leaving your creepy freakazoid cooties all over my chair."

I was so right in thinking all middle schools were alike. There were girls like her back at Brookdale. I once heard a rumor that some of them vowed to make at least one other girl cry every day.

Alyssa didn't cry, of course. Given the way she looked and her general attitude, I didn't doubt that she'd heard worse from kids here at school. Or on the street. Or maybe even from her own family.

She stared right back, unblinking, at the girl. Then she stood up, leaned over, and rubbed her hands all over the top of the desk.

"Now you've got cooties here too," she said, and sauntered off.

The girl turned to me, with the same pursed lips and squinted eyes. "Is she a friend of yours?" she demanded.

Fortunately, I didn't have to respond. We were distracted by the entrance of Ms. Gonzalez. Then the bell began to ring. And just before the clanging stopped, Rachel hurried in and managed to get to her desk on time.

From the other side of the room, Alyssa caught my eye and mouthed, "After class." I nodded.

Ms. Gonzalez addressed the class. "Today we begin our discussion of American poetry."

This announcement was met with a general groan. Ms. Gonzalez ignored it.

"Yes, my friends, over the next few weeks you will meet the likes of Langston Hughes. Carl Sandburg. Emily Dickinson. Li-Young Lee. And many others whom you may actually appreciate, believe it or not." She raised an eyebrow, as if daring us to comment further. "Today we'll begin with the great American literary figure Robert Frost," she said.

This was all good news to me. I'm not actually a huge poetry fan—I prefer stories that you can read and enjoy without worrying about symbolism and stuff. With poetry, you can't just appreciate it, you have to think about what it really *means*. At least, that's the way it was at Brookdale, so I was pretty sure it would be the same here.

But at least for today, I was pleased that we'd be reading Robert Frost, because I'd already done that, in October back at Brookdale. This meant I wouldn't have to pay too much attention today. I could think about the spyglass and what it might show me next. Or what it would show *us*—I was hoping that Alyssa might come home with me again today. And maybe that other girl, Rachel.

Which led me to think about what that mean girl had said. "Is she a friend of yours?" It's funny— much as I'd planned to be a loner here, I had to admit it was kind of nice having someone to talk with. Especially since there was something to talk *about*. Alyssa wasn't the kind of person I'd ever have been friends with back home, but maybe that was a good thing, considering what the friends back home had done to me.

Okay, so I'd pledged to myself that I wouldn't make any friends here. But Alyssa wasn't exactly what I'd call a friend, and she was a loner too. So I still wasn't completely breaking my vow.

"Kiara!"

Even though that wasn't my name, Ms. Gonzalez had spoken so loudly and sharply I looked up. She was addressing the girl who sat in front of me. The teacher strode down the aisle to the girl's desk and extended her hand.

"I told you what would happen if you continued to use that in class. Please give it to me."

I couldn't see the girl's face so I didn't know how she was reacting, but she didn't argue. Silently, she handed over the tablet.

"You can pick it up in the office after school," Ms. Gonzalez told her. "And if I see you with it again in class, Kiara, I'll call your parents."

"*Parent*," Kiara said. "*Singular.*"

"Well, I'll be calling her."

"Him," Kiara corrected.

Ms. Gonzalez nodded, and, with the tablet in hand, she returned to the front of the room.

I gazed at the back of Kiara's head with interest. Naturally, I'd known many kids with one parent, but in my experience that parent was usually a mother.

But I couldn't let myself wonder about her life, or daydream any longer about the spyglass and Alyssa. Clearly, Ms. Gonzalez had eagle eyes, and I didn't want her catching me not paying attention. So for what felt like the gazillionth time, I listened to a reading of "The Road Not Taken."

Although I was poised to leap from my desk the second the bell rang, there was no way Alyssa or I could catch Rachel. She was out of that room before either of us could leave our seats.

"It's okay," Alyssa assured me as we left the room

together. "We'll corner her at lunch. She always sits alone."

Sure enough, Rachel was the solitary occupant of a table in the cafeteria. As we stood in line for our food, Alyssa and I discussed our approach.

"I don't think we should tell her about the spy-glass right off," Alyssa said. "She'll think we're teasing her."

"Does she get bullied?" I asked.

"I never noticed," Alyssa admitted.

"I think we should just act like we're trying to make new friends," I suggested.

Alyssa frowned. "I don't know how to do that."

I shook my head wearily. "Just follow my lead."

As we walked through the cafeteria, I passed a table of boys, athletic types. A younger kid, most likely a sixth grader, carrying a tray of food, was walking past the table, and some jerk stuck out his leg to trip him. Another boy sitting at the table jumped up and caught the kid before he fell.

I recognized the good-deed boy. Mike Something. He was in my pre-algebra class, and I'd noticed him on my first first day. Mainly because he had red hair, which I love.

The smaller kid scurried away. "Hey, come on, Mike!" the jerky guy complained. He was clearly annoyed that Mike had spoiled his prank. But Mike just shook his head. "Not cool, Thayer." Then he sat back down at the table and joined the others in conversation.

I couldn't take my eyes off him. A nice guy sitting at a cool-guy table. Then he looked up and saw me. And he smiled!

Which didn't mean anything, of course. He was just being kind. And boys who were cool would never be interested in loner girls like me. I knew I could forget about any relationship like that here at East Lakeside.

As Alyssa and I approached Rachel's table, I could see that she wasn't eating school food like everyone else. She had little see-through containers of stuff—sliced fruit and what looked like a fancy salad.

When we stopped at the table, she glanced up. And we might as well have been zombies—she looked positively frightened.

"Mind if we join you?" I asked.

It took her a minute to respond.

"Why?"

"Just for company," I said. "I'm new here."

"We don't bite," Alyssa added.

Now Rachel looked even more alarmed, as if she was now actually considering that possibility.

She still hadn't given permission for us to join her, so I made a tentative gesture of pulling out a chair.

"Okay?" I asked.

It was only the tiniest of head movements, but I thought I saw her nod. So I sat down, and Alyssa did the same.

Rachel eyed us warily, and then she stuck a fork into her salad. A *real* fork, not a plastic one.

Alyssa couldn't take her eyes off the food. It did look really good. "You make your own lunch," she said. Given her tone, it sounded like an accusation.

"My mom makes it," Rachel murmured.

"Lucky you," I commented. "I'll bet it's a lot better than what we're eating. What's in the salad?"

"Tomato, avocado, and cucumber." Then she said, "Organic."

"Organic," I repeated. "You know, I see that word all the time but I don't know what it really means."

"It's all natural," Rachel explained softly. "No chemicals, no preservatives. My mothers only buy organic."

There was a moment of silence, and it took me a minute to think of a way to break it.

"I really liked your book report yesterday."

She eyed me suspiciously, and I thought about

the stupid boys in the class again. But I must have looked sincere, because she seemed to relax a little.

"Thank you."

"Now I want to read the book," I added.

She nodded. "It's really good."

"Have you ever read *Jane Eyre*?" I asked.

She nodded.

"That's my favorite book," I said.

"Yes, it's really good too."

Another silence. Alyssa was concentrating on her meal and not helping out with the conversation at all. Under the table, I kicked her lightly. She looked up.

"What?"

"We're discussing *Jane Eyre*," I said. "Do *you* have an opinion?"

She got the message. "Oh. Um, yeah, it's a pretty good book. But I prefer *Wuthering Heights*."

"I like that one too," Rachel said. Her voice was still barely above a whisper.

Alyssa was gazing at her with more interest now.

"Why are you so nervous?" she asked bluntly.

I wanted to kick her again, this time harder. It was way too soon to ask something so personal.

Alyssa hadn't been exaggerating when she said she knew nothing about making friends.

"I'm not nervous," Rachel whispered nervously.

But Alyssa didn't accept that. "Do kids pick on you?"

There was another one of those imperceptible nods.

"Because you don't fit in."

This nod was slightly more emphatic.

Alyssa nodded in satisfaction. "We don't fit in either."

The wariness in Rachel's expression was starting to fade. Encouraged, Alyssa continued.

"So maybe you would fit in with us."

Was that a glimmer of interest that I saw in Rachel's eyes?

"We're going over to my house after school today," I told her. "Just to hang out."

"And look at something interesting," Alyssa added. I shot her a warning look.

"Want to come?" I asked Rachel.

She seemed torn, and then she shook her head. "I can't. My mother is picking me up after school."

"Oh. Well, maybe tomorrow?"

Again Rachel shook her head. "She picks me up after school every day."

"Do you live far from school?" Alyssa asked.

"No, just over on Patton Drive."

"But that's within walking distance!" Alyssa exclaimed. "Why does your mother have to pick you up?"

"It's not with a car," Rachel explained. "My parents...they worry about me. Mom insists on walking me home from school."

She was blushing now, and with her fair skin, her face was practically beet red. I couldn't blame her for feeling embarrassed. It was one thing for an adult to meet you after school and walk you home when you were in elementary school. But in middle school? And it wasn't like Lakeside was crawling with dangerous elements.

Alyssa was clearly shocked by this news, and I tried to think of a way to change the subject before she could say anything to further humiliate Rachel.

"Do you call both your mothers Mom?" I asked.

"One of them is Mom. The other is Mami. She's from Mexico and that's how you say *Mom* in Spanish."

Alyssa wasn't giving up on the other subject so easily. "So maybe if *we* asked your mom, if she met us, she'd say okay and let you come."

Rachel looked doubtful, and I thought I knew why.

A lot of parents were probably not as open-minded as my mother, and Alyssa's style might not inspire confidence in the parent who picked Rachel up.

All around us, kids were getting up and carrying their trays over to the trash bins. I glanced at the clock and saw that lunch period was just about over.

Alyssa was waiting for Rachel to respond.

"Just think about it, okay?"

Rachel gave her another almost imperceptible nod.

We were all going in different directions to our next classes, so there was no more discussion. But I made a mental note to get to my locker before my last class and retrieve my coat so I could head outside directly when the bell rang. I thought that maybe Rachel's mother might approve of *me,* and I didn't want to miss her when she came to pick Rachel up.

My last class was a study period. I decided to go to the media center. We didn't have the Wi-Fi hooked up yet at home and I wanted to check my email. Not that I was expecting to hear from old friends back in Brookdale. If they weren't speaking to me, they wouldn't be writing or messaging me either. But it wouldn't hurt to check.

When I walked into the media center, I saw right

away that all the computer stations were occupied. So I wandered around and hoped someone would finish whatever they were doing and I could grab a place.

Then I recognized the back of one person's head—because in English class, I sat directly behind her. Kiara was leaning forward, her face practically attached to the screen she was facing. I paused and couldn't resist looking at it too.

She was playing some kind of game. I didn't recognize it, but then, I wasn't big on online gaming. There were times when I was bored and played single-player games, the kind where you shoot at stuff or match shapes and colors. But I would get to the point where I couldn't get through a round without spending money and I didn't have a credit card, so I just gave up.

What Kiara was playing didn't look like anything I'd seen before. Animated animal characters were moving around what looked like a labyrinth. Kiara hit a key, and a lightning bolt struck a bear and sent it to the other side.

I coughed loudly. She didn't react. So then I said, "Hi."

She turned. Her expression wasn't exactly friendly.

"What do you want?" she asked.

"I was just wondering how long you'll be using this computer."

"For the whole period," she replied, and turned back to the screen.

"Oh. Okay."

On the screen, a bird crashed into a swan, and Kiara groaned. Frantically, she hit some keys.

"What are you playing?" I asked.

She didn't even turn to me this time. "I don't think that's any of your business. And please stop spying on me."

"I wasn't spying," I protested. "Just looking."

"Same difference," she said.

"Sorry," I said, and backed away. Then I spotted an abandoned station and hurried over there.

As I'd expected, there weren't any emails, and I'd been unfriended and unfollowed so much on social media that I didn't even bother. I thought about actually doing homework, but I wasn't really in the mood. I couldn't stop thinking about Kiara.

six

AFTER SCHOOL, I RECOGNIZED RACHEL'S mother waiting outside the building. She was the same woman I'd seen through the spyglass when she was walking with Rachel. I realized then how much she looked like her daughter—pretty, curvy, and with Rachel's curly blond hair, only hers was cut shorter. I didn't approach her, though. She would wonder why I knew who she was, and I didn't want her to think I'd been spying on her.

Spying. I hadn't really thought that was what I'd been doing, but of course it was—that's why the telescope was called a spyglass. And it was what Kiara had accused me of doing in the media center, when she caught me looking at her game on the computer screen. Maybe spying wasn't a nice thing to do. But since the spyglass was showing me stuff that wasn't really there—didn't that make a difference?

But even if Kiara thought that was what I was doing, why did she react like that? Did she really not want to be friends?

Okay, true, *I'd* thought I wouldn't want any friends here at Lakeside, that I would be a loner and avoid any contact. But now, with Alyssa in my life, and maybe Rachel, I had to admit it was a good feeling to not be completely on my own. From what I'd seen of Kiara, she was definitely a loner. I guess I just couldn't figure why she wouldn't want that good feeling too.

I saw a warm smile cross Rachel's mother's face and I knew without even looking that Rachel must have emerged from the building. She walked directly to her mother, and I moved to intercept her.

"Hi, Rachel!" I said brightly, with the biggest smile I could muster.

"Hi," she said softly. It dawned on me that she might not remember my name, so I turned to her mother.

"I'm Ellie Marks. I'm in Rachel's English class."

The woman looked slightly surprised, and I got the feeling that no other student had ever spoken to Rachel in front of her here. But she smiled pleasantly.

"Hello, Ellie, I'm Jane Levin-Lopez, Rachel's mom." Then she turned to Rachel. "Ready to go?"

Rachel hesitated, and that encouraged me to speak up.

"Um, I was wondering if Rachel could come home with me."

Now Rachel's mom looked puzzled, so I quickly came up with a reason.

"To work on English homework together."

It was only a little white lie. We *did* have an assignment in English—to prepare oral reports on another Robert Frost poem we'd been given. But Rachel and I hadn't talked about working on this together.

Now her mother's brow furrowed. "Where do you live, Ellie?"

"Not far." I told her the address.

"Do I know your parents?" she asked.

"I don't think so. We just moved here."

"Will there be an adult at home?"

"Oh, sure." I should have said "probably," since there was a chance Mom could be at another interview and Dad could be out at a meeting.

She didn't look convinced, so I elaborated.

"My mother hasn't started working yet, and my father has his office at home. He's a lawyer," I added. I thought that would sound respectable.

Rachel's mom didn't seem reassured. Still, she didn't reject the proposal outright.

"Well, you live on the way to our house. We could stop there and I could meet your parents."

Wow. She was *really* protective. I tried to act like this was a natural request, and just hoped someone was home.

"Sure, we can do that." I glanced at Rachel, and she actually nodded, like she wanted to come!

Just then, Alyssa joined us. In her usual socially alienated manner, she didn't greet us. She just stood there, and my heart sank. One look at her skull earrings and Rachel's mother might think her daughter was being lured into something unpleasant. I could only hope that since I looked so boringly ordinary, that would make up for it.

Rachel finally spoke. "Mom, this is Alyssa. She's in our English class too."

I thought I saw a flash of apprehension on the woman's face. To my surprise, Alyssa actually made a small effort to be less alarming.

"Pleased to meet you," she said, and it was

audible! And she punctuated this with something closer to a real smile than I'd ever seen on her face.

Rachel's mother still didn't look convinced, but then Rachel piped up.

"Mom, I'd really like to go with them."

Ms. Levin-Lopez looked slightly surprised, and then her expression softened.

"Well... we'll see."

No one said much along the way. I commented on how mild the winter had been so far, and Alyssa said something about how we'd still get a snowstorm before it was over. But that was about it, and we walked the rest of the way in silence.

When we reached my house, they joined me on the steps. It was a relief when the door opened without my having to use a key. Someone had to be home.

"Mom? Dad?" I called.

My mother came down the stairs. "Hi, honey."

I beckoned for the others to come in.

"Mom, you remember Alyssa. This is Rachel, and this is..."

"I'm Jane Levin-Lopez," Rachel's mother said, extending a hand to shake.

"Lisa Marks," Mom said, and shook her hand. "Happy to meet you."

"Your daughter invited mine over to do home-work together," Ms. Levin-Lopez said. "I just wanted to make sure there would be an adult in the house."

"Of course. And I'm very pleased that Ellie's making new friends."

I winced. I could almost hear "I told you so" in her words.

Mom offered Rachel's mother coffee, but she said she had to get home.

"I do graphic design, and I've got a job due at the end of the week." She looked at her watch and then spoke to Rachel.

"I'll pick you up at five-thirty," she said, and Rachel nodded. Then Ms. Levin-Lopez went into her handbag and took out a business card, which she handed to my mother.

"This has my phone number, if there's any problem."

With one last affectionate-but-worried look at her daughter, Ms. Levin-Lopez left. My mother addressed us all.

"You girls must be hungry. There's no cake left, but help yourselves to whatever you can find in the kitchen. I've got some phone calls to make." She went back upstairs.

Rachel looked at me in awe. "She lets you fix your own snacks?"

"Sure, why not?"

Rachel didn't answer. Alyssa and I exchanged looks, and I was sure we were both thinking the same thing—that either the Ms. Levin-Lopez we'd met or the other Ms. Levin-Lopez prepared everything Rachel could eat. I wondered if we could find anything organic in my kitchen.

But it seemed that Rachel on her own didn't have any real commitment to eating organically. Raiding the cabinets and the refrigerator, we found a big bag of potato chips, a sack of chocolate chip cookies, and a large bottle of soda, and she didn't offer any objections. I added cups and napkins, and we took the haul upstairs.

I'd decided we should get to know Rachel better before we showed her the spyglass. She was such a sheltered kid, something magical could totally freak her out. So I led the girls into my bedroom, where we settled down on the rug and spread out the goodies.

Again, Rachel seemed to be in awe as she looked over the snacks. It was like she'd never seen junk food before.

"I don't think any of this stuff's organic," I told her.

"That's okay," Rachel assured me. She offered a shy smile. "But I probably won't tell my parents about this."

"Just pretend it's carrot sticks and apple juice," Alyssa advised.

We all began eating, including Rachel, who seemed particularly enamored of the cookies.

I was curious. "So your mothers are pretty strict about what you eat, huh?"

"They worry about my health," Rachel said.

"Have you been sick? Do you have allergies?"

"Nope. They just worry about everything when it comes to me."

"All parents worry," Alyssa remarked.

"Not like mine," Rachel said.

"I guess I'm lucky that way," Alyssa declared.

I looked at her in surprise. After all I'd heard about her family, it was startling to hear Alyssa describe herself as lucky.

She explained. "They're super busy all the time and there are four kids in our house, so they have to divide up the worrying. Are you an only child?"

"Yes. Well, yes and no," Rachel replied. "There *was* another child. But she died."

I'd been stuffing my face with chips and Alyssa had been working on the cookies, but we both stopped eating at this news. We stared at Rachel in shock.

I could barely get words out. "Your sister died?"

"Before I was born," Rachel told them. "She was ten years old. Walking home from school, she was hit by a car."

"Oh, wow," Alyssa murmured. "That's so tragic."

Rachel nodded. "She was alone when it happened."

Now something made sense to me. "So that's why your mom walks you home from school."

"She walks me there too. Well, either her or Mami. Usually Mom, because she works from home. But the two of them, they barely let me out of their sight. I know kids at school have noticed, and I know they laugh at me. But what can I do?"

"Your parents are afraid of losing you too," I said softly.

"Exactly. So they treat me like I'm five years old." Rachel sighed. "Sometimes I *feel* like I'm five years old."

"Do you *wish* you were five years old?" I asked.

"No!"

Interesting, I thought. So it wasn't just wishes or

fantasies that the spyglass was showing us. It was *feelings* too.

Alyssa and I exchanged meaningful looks. The moment had come to tell Rachel.

"We've got something to show you," I said.

seven

"A TELESCOPE?" UP IN THE TURRET, RACHEL looked at the object with interest.

"We call it a spyglass," Alyssa said.

"Because...you use it to spy on people?"

"Sort of," I told her.

"But not exactly," Alyssa added. "Like, we don't look in people's windows to see them taking their clothes off or anything like that."

"It's a different kind of spying," I said. "It's kind of hard to explain. We see stuff that...well, stuff that's not really there."

Alyssa shook her head. "No, what we see *is* really there, in a way. But other people can't see it."

Rachel looked confused. "You mean you have to have a spyglass to see this stuff?"

"Not just any spyglass," I said. "This one...it's special."

Rachel looked at it. "So this one's more powerful?"

"No, it's not that," I began, trying to think of a way to explain it. Alyssa took over.

"It's magic."

Now Rachel was clearly dubious. And uncomfortable. She started to back away. "I don't believe in magic."

"Neither do we!" I declared. Then I glanced at Alyssa. "Well, I mean, I don't. Or, I didn't. But now... well, it's hard to explain. What we see is what people want. Or think about."

"Or feel," Alyssa added. "Like, when you just said sometimes you feel like you're five years old—"

"Wait," I interrupted. This could totally boggle Rachel's mind.

I thought we should give some other examples first, to prepare her. So I described seeing the community center and then finding out that it wasn't even built yet.

"And then Ellie saw me, on a broomstick. Flying."

"Oh, come on," Rachel protested.

"*I* believe her! Because, see, sometimes I feel like a witch. My stepsister called me a witch. I'll bet half the kids at school think I'm a witch. And then, yesterday, we saw *you*."

"What was I doing?" Rachel asked her.

"Walking with your mom. The one we just met."

"So what? I do that all the time."

"You looked like you were about five years old."

Rachel stared at her in disbelief. I jumped in.

"See, like I said, we think the spyglass is showing us our feelings. Alyssa's father told her people have been wanting a community center for ages."

Alyssa explained. "Because a lot of people can't afford to belong to fancy country clubs. And a lot of high school kids have nothing to do."

"And like Alyssa said, she thinks about being a witch, what it would be like to have powers like that," I said. "And then, just now, you were saying you sometimes feel like a little kid around your parents. Well, that's how we saw you. Like a little kid. Through the spyglass."

Rachel still looked skeptical, but she asked, "Can I look through it?"

"Sure!" I exclaimed eagerly. I showed her how to operate the dial to magnify the view, and she took her place behind the eyepiece.

After a minute, Alyssa asked, "Well? What do you see?"

"School. Town Hall." Rachel moved the spyglass a little. "A church. The high school. Cars. People walking." She turned to look at us severely. "None of them are flying."

"Keep looking," I urged.

After another few seconds, she said, "Nothing unusual." She looked at us again. "Are you sure you're not just imagining this stuff?"

Alyssa shook her head. "Okay, only Ellie saw the community center and me on the broomstick. But we both saw *you*. And we weren't talking about you or anything. How could we both be imagining the same thing at the same time?"

"And it's not like we have anything in common," I added. "Alyssa and I just met a couple of days ago."

"Have you seen other kids from school?" Rachel asked me.

I shook my head.

"Why just me and Alyssa?"

"I don't know," I admitted. "Unless, maybe..." I bit my lower lip.

"What?" Alyssa demanded.

I hesitated, but I plunged in. "Well, maybe we do have something in common. We're all kind of outsiders, aren't we? I mean, we don't really fit in." I eyed them nervously, hoping they wouldn't take this as an insult.

Apparently not. Alyssa nodded, and Rachel didn't disagree.

"So...maybe we're special." It was a weak explanation, I knew that. But I couldn't think of anything else to say.

"But you haven't seen yourself, have you?" Rachel pointed out.

I shrugged. "Maybe one of you will. Someday."

"I'll look again," Rachel said, turning back to the spyglass. "Okay, I see...Mike Twersky."

The name rang a bell. "Who's that?"

"A boy at school. Red hair, cute. Kind of nice."

With the description, I immediately knew who she was talking about. "Oh, yeah, he's in my pre-algebra class. What's he doing?"

"Shooting hoops on someone's carport with a couple of other boys."

Well, that was too bad. If he'd been doing something weird, it might have provided me with a reason to speak to him. Like Rachel said, he was awfully cute.

"What else?" Alyssa asked.

"Hmm...a car just ran a red light. And now a

police car is pulling him over." After a few seconds, she said, "Uh-oh, someone's going to get a ticket."

This was getting boring. I was beginning to wonder if we'd been wrong to bring Rachel up here. The spyglass wasn't offering her anything.

"Must be something good at the movie theater. There's a line."

Alyssa yawned.

"I see Kiara, from our English class, on the playground. She's running..." Rachel's voice trailed off, and she drew in her breath sharply.

"What?" I asked. "What's happening?"

Rachel moved back from the spyglass. Her normally pale face was practically white. And she couldn't speak. I stepped into her place.

I could see Kiara too. And she wasn't alone. Running alongside and around her were...a donkey, a large tiger, and a gorilla. They were playing tag.

"Let me see!" Alyssa demanded.

I turned the spyglass over to her.

"Holy cannoli," she breathed.

I turned to Rachel. Her face was returning to its natural color, but she still looked stunned.

"Did you...did you see...," she stuttered.

I nodded. "I saw."

Then Alyssa let out a yelp. "Look!" She stepped

aside and let me see. Kiara was gone. Her place had been taken by a gigantic swan.

I gave Rachel her chance. "I don't understand," she said. "What does it mean? Kiara wants to be a swan?"

Suddenly, the pieces started falling into place. "Oh my gosh," I said excitedly. "You know what? I think it's the game she plays!"

"What game?" Alyssa asked.

"I don't know what it's called but she was playing it on a computer in the media center today. And I saw animals like those running around on the screen."

Then Rachel said, "It's over. Now it's just Kiara, and she's all by herself." She moved away. Alyssa and I both took a look and confirmed this.

"So, I guess now you believe us?" Alyssa asked Rachel.

Slowly, Rachel nodded. "Only...I still don't get it."

But we didn't have a chance to discuss this latest vision from the spyglass. A voice came from the floor below.

"Ellie? Where are you?"

"Up here, Mom!"

I could hear her coming up the stairs, and a second later she ran into the turret.

"I have news! I got the job!"

"Mom, that's great!" If the other girls hadn't been there, I would have hugged her, so I tried to compensate by putting tons of enthusiasm in my voice.

"What are you going to do?" Rachel asked.

"I'll be a reporter for the county newspaper, covering business—plus I'm going to be writing a weekly column!"

"What's it going to be about?" I asked.

"Oh, pretty much anything and everything, as long as it's entertaining and interesting for the community."

Her eyes were sparkling, and I couldn't remember the last time I'd seen her so excited. She beamed at us.

"Ellie, I want to celebrate and your father's got clients coming. So how about I take you girls out to the Lakeside Diner for super-delicious hot fudge sundaes?"

Alyssa and I quickly agreed, but Rachel looked at her watch.

"It's after five. My mom will be coming for me."

"Why don't I call her and tell her I'll drop you off at your home after we go to the diner?" my mother suggested. "You girls go gather your coats and I'll meet you at the door."

But when we all converged downstairs, my mother was shaking her head regretfully. "I'm sorry, Rachel. Your mother wants you home now, so I'll have to drop you on our way."

Rachel didn't look devastated. A small sigh was the only indication of any disappointment. It was like she'd expected this.

"It's okay. She means well."

If this had happened to me—if my mother had said I couldn't do something and there was no good reason for it—I would have thrown a fit and gotten into an argument with her. The friends I used to know, they would have done the same.

Rachel...she just gave in. And what would Alyssa do, I wondered. Probably just ignore her parents' demands and do what she wanted to do.

The friends I was making here...they were certainly different. But I had to admit, this was making my new life interesting.

Along with the spyglass, of course.

eight

ON SATURDAY MORNING, I RAN DOWN THE stairs in a panic and stormed into the kitchen, where I confronted my parents drinking coffee at the breakfast table.

"We still don't have internet!" I cried in dismay. I'd been planning to do my English homework today, but I'd left my textbook in my locker at school. Now I couldn't even look up the dumb Robert Frost poem online, and our oral reports were due on Monday.

"I know, it's a pain," my mother said. "I called the

cable company again yesterday, and they said the guy should be here on Monday, maybe Tuesday."

"Tuesday?" I shrieked. "I need internet now! I've got homework!"

My parents exchanged looks, and my father shook his head wearily.

"Honey, it's not all about you! We're all dealing with this. Do you think I like having to go to a coffee shop with my laptop to send emails?"

"You could write and send emails on your phone," I pointed out. My parents had smartphones, unlike me. Mine is only good for calls and texts, no apps, no email.

Dad shook his head. "Kiddo, you know I can't type on that tiny phone keypad. So going to a place with internet is what I have to do right now. And you'll just have to find another way to do your homework for the next three days."

"Then can I use one of your phones?" I asked. "*I* can deal with those tiny keyboards." But I knew the answer would be no. My parents are big on personal privacy. I just hope they remember that when I get a smartphone of my own.

As I expected, they both shook their heads. "I'm sure the library has computers you can use," my mother said.

"It's Saturday, Mom," I countered. "School isn't open. And for your information, we don't call it a library, it's a media center."

"I was referring to the public library," she replied calmly.

"The big building with the columns on Main Street," Dad added.

"I know where it is, thank you very much," I replied, my voice dripping with sarcasm.

Now both their expressions became grim. It was time to get out of there.

Back in Brookdale, I was a regular at the public library. I like to read, and former-best-friend Lily and I used to go there every Saturday morning to check out books. But here in Lakeside, for the past week, there'd been so much going on that I hadn't even finished the paperback I bought just before we moved. It was one of those stories about terrible future worlds. In this one, teens were killing each other to get more food, and I thought it would be helpful to read about people whose lives were more depressing than mine. But it had been slow going and I was ready to give up on it. Probably because, so far, my life here hadn't been as depressing as I thought it would be.

So I needed something new to read for pleasure,

and I needed internet. I wouldn't admit this to my mom, but she was right, it was time to discover the Lakeside Public Library.

If I had to say one thing about Lakeside that made it better than Brookdale, it would be the fact that the public library here was within walking distance. I didn't have to wait around for someone to find the time to drive me there.

Brookdale's library was an ugly low brick building with windows that always looked dirty. A storm had broken off one of the letters in the name over the door, and no one ever got around to fixing it, so the building name was B OOKDALE PUBLIC LIBRARY, which I actually thought was kind of appropriate.

But Lakeside's library was really impressive—white, with columns, and all the letters of the name were there, emblazoned in gold over the entrance. When I walked in, I was immediately hit with that special musty library smell. I always liked that smell, and I used to think they should make a perfume like that. It probably wouldn't attract any romance, but it would make me feel happy.

I didn't go directly to the computers. I knew there wouldn't be any emails, other than ads for all the stuff I'd liked on Facebook. As for Snapchat and Instagram and all the rest—I didn't particularly want to see what the kids I used to know were up to. And maybe it was that tantalizing smell that drove me directly into the stacks.

It also dawned on me that I didn't need internet to find the Robert Frost poem I'd been assigned to write about. I could just find it in a book of Robert Frost poems—which I did, easily. And then, on Alyssa's recommendation, I picked up a copy of *Wuthering Heights*.

I went to the checkout line, and someone I recognized got into the line right behind me. Suddenly, I had a hard time breathing.

"Hi," I managed to say.

He looked at me blankly.

"I'm Ellie Marks. We're in the same pre-algebra class."

He nodded. "Oh, yeah. I'm Mike Twersky."

Like I didn't already know that.

Without even thinking, I blurted out a stupid question. "What are you doing here?"

He indicated the object in his hand. "Checking out a book."

"Oh. Yeah," I said. "Me too." And then I added, "Two books."

He nodded.

I smiled.

End of my fabulous connection with a very cute guy.

At least, I thought it was the end. Mike walked out of the building behind me just as someone walking in bumped into him and knocked his book out of his hand. It dropped down a couple of steps and landed right in front of me.

I picked it up and couldn't help glancing at the title. *Birds of North America*. I handed it back to him.

"Thanks," he said, and tossed it into his backpack.

"You're welcome," I responded. "Are you into birds?"

I expected him to say it was for someone else, a sibling, a parent. Or maybe he had to write a report about birds.

He nodded. "Um, well...yeah. Watching them."

I was impressed. Bird watching was definitely not among the popular activities for kids our age. Not the cool ones, at least, and Mike Twersky had to be one of them. Bird watching was like playing golf, something old retired folks did. It wasn't just the fact that he did this that impressed me. He admitted it!

"Wow," I said. "That's—cool."

He looked at me suspiciously, as if he thought I might be speaking sarcastically.

"No, really!" I said quickly. "I like birds." Which wasn't exactly a lie. I didn't *dislike* them. I just hadn't given them much thought.

His expression cleared. "That's what I'm going to do now. You know the little kids' playground, just by the woods? It's a great place to spot birds."

"That's good to know," I said. "I mean, in case I decide to take up bird watching. Which I might. Someday."

"Want to come with me?"

Well, Robert Frost could wait.

I couldn't believe I was actually walking side by side with Mike Twersky. I wondered what would happen if we ran into people from school, like some of the popular girls. Would he introduce me? Would they be impressed by the fact that I was hanging with a popular boy?

Pushing that thought from my mind, I scolded myself. Why would I care if kids from the popular crowd were impressed or not? I'd sworn off those girls, I knew what they were like. Lakeside was not going to turn into another Brookdale for me.

On the other hand, I hadn't sworn off popular *boys*.

We walked in silence. I tried to come up with something to talk about, but as it turned out, I didn't need to. Mike's cell phone rang, and he took it out of his pocket.

"Hey, Thayer."

The name was familiar, and I remembered where I'd heard it—he was the guy who tripped the smaller boy in the cafeteria. He must have been a good friend of Mike's—they stayed on the phone the whole time we walked. It was kind of weird to think that Mike could be friends with a creepy bully type like that. On the other hand, I'd had friends who'd turned out to be not so nice.

Thayer was also a very talkative friend. Mike's side of the conversation consisted mostly of "Yeah," "Right," "No way," "Sure," and "Okay."

My cell phone didn't ring. I'd gotten it for Christmas, and since I no longer had any friends calling me, or any friends to call, and since it wasn't a smartphone, I'd mainly used it for setting the alarm to get up in the mornings. Thinking about that, I realized I didn't even know if Alyssa and Rachel had cell phones. If they did, they hadn't received or made any calls when we'd been together. Maybe it was time to actually add some names to my contacts.

It was a nice playground, with all the usual stuff—swings, a slide, a seesaw, and a pretty merry-go-round with painted horses. But it was very cold out, so the area was deserted. Mike set his backpack on a bench and opened it. He took out the book about birds and then pulled out binoculars. I stood there silently while he flipped through the book.

"Here are some birds we might be able to see in the winter," he said, and held out the book so I could see the pictures. All the birds looked pretty much the same to me, but I pretended to study them carefully and faked some enthusiasm.

"Wow! A white-breasted nuthatch!" I exclaimed, and then immediately wanted to kick myself. *Breast. Nut.* How could I use words like that in front of a guy? I gritted my teeth and waited for the teasing.

But all he said was "Yeah, I'd like to see one of those. They're not very common, but it's possible."

He held the binoculars to his eyes and searched the skies. Some birds flew out of the woods.

"Anything interesting?" I asked.

"Just pigeons."

He continued to look around, and every time a bird flew he aimed his binoculars in that direction. He didn't say anything, so I figured they weren't very exciting birds.

I wished he would ask me something about myself, like where did I come from, or how I liked Lakeside. But we didn't really know each other, so maybe he thought questions would be too personal. My mother once told me that boys my age get nervous around girls, which is why they might not be very talkative. Especially if the boys were attracted to the girls. So I guess it was a good thing that Mike didn't say much. Except Mike really didn't seem nervous at all. Still, he was a boy.

Suddenly, he let out a whoop. "I think that's a white-winged crossbill!"

"Is that a rare bird?" I asked.

"Not rare, exactly, but not real common."

He handed me the binoculars. "Look, over there. It's circling around the fir tree."

I looked. There was definitely a bird, but I didn't notice anything remarkable about it. Still, I exclaimed, "Cool!" I handed the binoculars back to him and he looked again.

"It's coming this way!" he exclaimed, and raised the binoculars.

I had a sudden memory of being in a park one day when a bunch of birds flew over me and one of them pooped right on my head. It was totally disgusting. Fortunately, Mike's white-winged crossbill had better manners.

"Could you hand me the bird book, please?" he asked. "I want to check it off."

I did. He flipped through some pages, took a pen out of his pocket, then smiled and put it back.

"For a second there I forgot it's a library book," he admitted.

Wow, *that* was impressive. A lot of people wouldn't care about defacing a library book.

"Those binoculars are heavy," I commented.

"Yeah, all the really good ones are," he said. "I got these for Christmas."

"Can you do bird watching through a..." I almost said "spyglass," but that sounded too much like something in a fairy tale. "Through a telescope?"

"Sure," he said. He looked at me curiously. "Why? Do you have a telescope?"

"Yeah. Well, it's not exactly mine. I found it in the turret at home, just after we moved in." I hesitated, then added, "You can come over sometime, if you want, and look through it."

Was I being too aggressive? He didn't look frightened.

"Yeah, maybe. Thanks."

To be honest, the idea made me a little nervous. Would he see something other than birds? It was one thing to share my magic spyglass with my new odd friends. But a cool guy like Mike? Would he think I was weird?

He looked at his watch. "Oh, I gotta go, my grandparents are coming for lunch. See ya."

"See ya," I repeated as he put his backpack on and took off.

See ya, I repeated silently to myself. Did that mean he *wanted* to see me? That if we saw each other at school, we'd speak? I felt dazed. My head was spinning, in a very nice way.

Maybe that was why it took me a minute to realize that the playground was no longer completely deserted. Someone in a parka with a hood was sitting on one of the swings, listlessly swaying back and forth. A wind blew back the hood and revealed Kiara Douglas.

Since I was the only other person on the playground, I felt certain that she must have seen me, but she didn't wave or give any sign of recognition. I strolled over, sat down on the swing next to hers, and spoke.

"Hi."

She glanced in my direction but didn't return the greeting. Surely she recognized me, after our encounter in the media center. Even so, I introduced myself.

"I'm Ellie. I sit behind you in English."

"I *know,*" she said, in a tone that was less than happy.

Still, at least she *spoke*.

"It's cold," I said.

"I *know*," she said again.

"Too cold to be outside," I remarked.

"Then why are you?" she asked.

An actual question! I took that as encouragement, and I responded.

"I was bird watching."

She made no comment about that, so I followed up with a question of my own.

"Why are *you* outside in the cold?"

"My father ordered me to get some fresh air."

I nodded. "Well, it's getting a little too fresh for me, if you know what I mean."

Was that a nod of agreement? I couldn't be sure.

"I think I'll go home and make some hot chocolate."

No response.

"Want to come?" I asked.

There was no mistaking the confused expression on her face. "Why?"

"Just, you know, for company. I'm new here and I'm trying to make some friends."

She stared at me in silence for at least ten seconds. Then she spoke.

"I've already got friends."

I couldn't help myself, I had to get personal. "You do? That's interesting. Because I never see you hanging with anyone at school. You're always alone."

"My friends aren't at East Lakeside Middle School."

"They go to another school?"

"I guess."

How could she not know where her friends went to school? I was about to ask her that when she spoke again.

"PonyGirl," she said. "FunkyMonkey. Turkey TwentyTwo. Those are only some of my friends. I don't need more." And she hopped off the swing and walked away.

nine

I DIDN'T WORK ON MY ROBERT FROST POEM Saturday night. After my encounter with Mike Twersky that afternoon, I had absolutely no desire to concentrate on poetic words and try to figure out their inner meaning. Maybe if it had been a love poem, I would have found it more interesting.

Fortunately, my parents were going out, so I didn't have to hide in my room and pretend to be working. As soon as they left, I went into a certain closet where Mom and Dad had tossed a lot of stuff they never used anymore, like their skis and old

DVDs. It was so weird to think they had been young once, but these DVDs were evidence of that. I picked out two with covers I liked—*The Breakfast Club* and *Grease.*

In the end, I had a very nice evening stuffing my face with popcorn and zoning out, but that meant I had to attack Robert Frost on Sunday. Late in the morning, I opened the book I'd checked out of the library and found the poem I'd been assigned.

It was called "Fire and Ice," and I was very pleased to see that it wasn't long at all. How much symbolism and inner meaning could be packed into nine short lines? I was even more pleased when I read it through and found it easy to understand. It was all about how the world could end, in fire or in ice. Robert Frost says he'd go with fire, but then he says ice would work too.

Not a complicated poem, but my heart sank. I could sum it up in three seconds. How was I going to talk about it for five full minutes?

Ms. Gonzalez said we had to relate the poem to our own lives. So I figured I should talk about how *I* thought the world would end. Which was not something I'd ever thought about.

Now I tried to think about it. I saw a movie once where an atomic bomb fell and everyone was slowly dying of radiation poisoning. Radiation—that would be sort of like fire.

I groaned aloud at the idea. This was so depressing! Here I was, finally feeling sort of okay about life—this poem was going to really bring me down. I put the book aside and went downstairs to see what we were having for lunch.

"Cold roast beef," my father informed me as he perused the refrigerator contents. "Leftover chicken."

"And there's coleslaw and veggies," my mother added. Then, to me, she said, "Did you finish your homework?"

"Just about," I lied. And then I had an inspiration. "You know, this English thing we have to do is an oral report. Could I ask Alyssa and Rachel to come over after lunch so we can practice the reports on each other?"

I got permission and ran upstairs to retrieve my cell phone. Then I remembered—I didn't have their phone numbers. I went back downstairs.

My mother was putting platters of food on the kitchen table. "Are they coming?"

"I couldn't call them, I don't have their numbers. And there's no internet to look them up, remember?"

"I still have Jane Levin-Lopez's card on the

refrigerator," Mom said. "I think it has her cell and home numbers on it."

"Okay...but what about Alyssa?"

"Four-one-one," my father said.

"Huh?"

"You call information. You dial four-one-one, you give the name, and you get a phone number."

"There *was* information available before the internet, El," my mother pointed out. "When we were your age—"

"Okay, okay, I get it," I interrupted. "Can I get cell phone numbers through four-one-one?"

"Usually just landlines," she said. "So it'll probably be under her parents' name."

I thought about that for a minute. There had to be more than one Parker in town—except, I remembered, Alyssa's mom had a different last name from her daughter. Khatri. And her stepfather probably wasn't a Parker.

I decided to try her mom's name. I dialed 411 and gave the name. No luck. Then I remembered something Alyssa told me.

"Dad, do you know the name of the architect who's building the community center?"

"Martin Kraft."

I tried again—and it worked! I called the number 411 gave me and Alyssa answered the phone herself.

"Hi!" I replied. "It's Ellie. Want to come over this afternoon and practice our oral reports?"

"Not particularly," she replied. "I wouldn't mind coming over, but I don't want to practice this stupid report."

With my parents able to overhear me, I decided to ignore that. "Great," I said. "Two-thirty?"

"And we'll do something else?"

"Absolutely."

Rachel's home phone was answered by a woman who didn't sound like the mother I'd met. Probably her other mother.

"Could I speak to Rachel, please?"

"May I ask who is calling?"

"This is her friend Ellie. From East Lakeside."

There was a moment of silence, and then I caught a whispered conversation but couldn't hear what anyone was saying. I imagined this parent—the one Rachel called Mami—was asking the other mother if she knew who I was. She must have said she did, because her Mami spoke again.

"Yes, one moment, please."

Finally, Rachel herself was on the phone, and I repeated my invitation. She asked me to wait, and

I presumed she was asking permission. Then she came back.

"Are your parents going to be home?"

I did a mental eye roll. Poor Rachel. "Yeah, I guess so."

Rachel lowered her voice. "Better find out for sure. One of them will drive me over and she'll probably want to see that someone's there."

I sighed. "Hang on." I turned to them. "You guys home today?"

I got a couple of nods and was able to report to Rachel that adult supervision was available. Like we were all really five years old and needed it.

That afternoon, Alyssa walked over, and just as I opened the door, a car pulled up to the curb. Rachel and her other mother got out.

"Mom," I called.

While my mother and Ms. Levin-Lopez talked, the girls and I went up to the turret.

"Are we going to practice our reports now?" Rachel asked.

"Later," I said. "First I have to tell you about Kiara." I reported my meeting with her on the playground the day before.

Alyssa frowned. "FunkyMonkey?"

"Yeah, and Ponygirl, and another name I can't

remember," I said. "I'm thinking they might be characters in the game she plays."

Rachel looked puzzled. "So they're not real people?"

"No, they're avatars," I told her. "So they *are* real people, but I don't think Kiara actually knows them. It's an online game, they could be anywhere in the world."

"And she calls them her friends?" Rachel shook her head. "That's weird."

"*She's* weird," I declared.

Alyssa shrugged. "I don't know. Everybody's weird, in my opinion. *We're* weird."

I couldn't argue with that. "Maybe we'll see her today," I said, and went to the spyglass. I slowly moved it around town.

"See anything?" Alyssa asked.

"The parking lot at school. And it's full of cars."

"That's impossible," Rachel noted. "It's Sunday."

"I know!" I was excited. "Maybe we're going to see something interesting. Wait—there are two people coming out of the building. They're going into the parking lot." I turned the dial so I could see their faces. "Hey, one of them is Mr. Clark!"

"Our science teacher?" said Rachel incredulously.

"Yeah. I don't know the other one, but I've seen her around, she's a teacher too."

"Let me see!" Alyssa begged.

Reluctantly, I handed it over.

"Oh, yeah, that's Ms. Hannigan! She teaches art." Then she shrieked.

"What?" Rachel and I said in unison.

"They're *dancing*!"

Sure enough, as we each took a turn viewing, we saw that Ms. Hannigan had a hand on Mr. Clark's shoulder, Mr. Clark's hand was on her waist, their other hands were clasped, and they were doing some kind of slow dance. Right in the middle of the parking lot.

"Do you think they're a couple?" Rachel wondered.

Alyssa shook her head. "They must *want* to be a couple. The spyglass shows us feelings and wishes, remember? I'll bet they each have a secret crush on the other."

"Hey, maybe we could bring them together!" I exclaimed. "Like in *Clueless*!"

They both looked at me blankly. Obviously, their parents didn't have a stash of old teen movies like mine did.

"It's probably on streaming. And I've got the DVD." I had a wistful memory of sleepovers back in Brookdale with former friends. Pajamas and popcorn in front of the TV. "Hey, maybe you two can come over sometime, stay overnight, and we can watch it."

I could tell from Rachel's expression that she'd never been to a sleepover.

"Do you think your parents would let you?" I asked her.

She considered this. "Maybe...and maybe I could beg."

"Or insist?" Alyssa asked.

Rachel considered that. "Um...maybe."

I wanted to hug her.

"Good for you," Alyssa declared. "Do what you want to do. Forget them. Fight for your rights."

"I'm not sure I'm ready to do that," Rachel murmured as Alyssa went back to the spyglass.

"Anything interesting?" I asked.

"Paige Nakamura."

The name was familiar. "Who's that?"

"Remember the girl in English class who didn't want to catch my cooties?"

Rachel shook her head sadly. "Why are mean girls like that so popular? I don't get it."

"Maybe she's not so popular," Alyssa commented. "She's all alone and she's crying."

"For real?" I asked.

"Couldn't be," Alyssa replied. "She's not wearing a coat and it's freezing outside."

I took a look. Sure enough, there were leaves on the trees. It wasn't winter in the spyglass. I let Rachel look.

"I guess even popular girls can have problems," Rachel commented. "I wonder why she's crying."

"I don't know and it's not important," Alyssa stated. "She deserves problems, the way she picks on people, and not just me. She makes really awful cracks. Not that I care," she added hastily.

I wondered if that was really true. Thinking back, I remembered how hurt I felt when kids started saying mean things to me.

Rachel sighed. "I know, she's made fun of me too. Sometimes I wonder what's worse: getting insulted and being called names, or just being ignored."

I was ignored too, back at Brookdale, when friends stopped speaking to me. Like Rachel, I didn't know which was worse.

"Let's look for Kiara," I suggested.

We surveyed the town, but all we saw this time was the real Lakeside on a Sunday afternoon.

"Why are you so interested in her?" Rachel asked.

"Because I think she might be one of us," I said. "You know. A loner." Even as I said this, I was thinking that we're not really loners anymore. We have each other.

But Alyssa and Rachel seemed to know what I was saying.

"We should find out more about this game she plays," Alyssa said. "We maybe could understand her better. Can we look it up now?"

I groaned. "We don't have internet yet. Maybe not till Tuesday."

Rachel piped up. "Why don't you two come to my house tomorrow after school and we can try to find her game? Bring your phones or a laptop. Maybe we can join it."

Alyssa and I agreed to this. And then Rachel suggested practicing our oral reports.

Alyssa frowned. "I thought we weren't really going to do that."

"I haven't even worked on mine," I confessed.

But Rachel had, and wanted to talk about it. "I'm a little nervous about it," she told us. "You know how Ms. Gonzalez said we had to make the report personal? I'm worried about talking like that in front of the class." She turned to Alyssa. "Do you know what you're going to say?"

"Yeah, kind of. My poem is 'Stopping by Woods on a Snowy Evening.'"

"What's it about?" I asked.

"There's this guy, and he wants to go into the beautiful winter woods, to, like, be in that environment and experience it, but in the end he doesn't because he's got other stuff to do. Responsibilities." She hesitated, and then she said, "So I'm going to talk about how one time I thought I'd run away from home, to get away from my family. Who probably wouldn't even notice that I was gone." She sighed. "But I didn't. I mean, who knows? They might have noticed and completely freaked out."

"Wow." I was impressed. That was pretty personal. "What's yours?" I asked Rachel.

Rachel's poem was "Desert Places." It was about someone being isolated. In her report, which she delivered to us right then and there, she talked about how she could relate to the poem, because she felt very lonely sometimes.

"That's brave," Alyssa commented when she was done.

"I know some kids might laugh," Rachel said. "They'll think I'm a real loser."

I put an arm around her. "Well, you're not a loser. And who cares what they think? We'll be there to support you. You've got friends."

Alyssa nodded in agreement. And Rachel looked like she was going to cry.

She didn't, though. Instead, we went downstairs and dug up some snacks. Rachel's Mami—who turned out to be called Cecilia Levin-Lopez—was still there, talking to my mother, and fortunately, they were so involved in their conversation that Rachel's Mami didn't notice that we were eating nonorganic corn chips.

Once everyone was gone, my mother asked how the practice went.

"Okay," I said. "But I've got a little more work to do." And I ran up to my room.

I felt ashamed. Alyssa and Rachel had really worked on their poems, and they were both relating the poems to their own lives in especially meaning-ful ways. I had to come up with something. And not how I thought the world would end.

Reading the poem over a couple more times, I thought about what the poet was really saying. It was something about what was worse, fire or ice. And then I remembered what Rachel had said earlier. Which was worse, getting picked on or being ignored?

Getting picked on, that's fire. It's a real attack, it's hot, and it burns. Ice...that's freezing. And when people stop speaking to you, when they stop being your friends, it's like they freeze you out. I'd been through both back at Brookdale. So had my parents.

I started making notes for my talk.

ten

IT WASN'T TOO AWFUL IN ENGLISH THE NEXT day. While I gave my report, most of the kids looked bored, but that was okay because that was how they looked during all the reports. A couple of kids actually looked sort of interested, but I was glad they didn't make any comments or ask any questions after I finished. I didn't really want to go into any more detail about what happened in Brookdale.

Poor Rachel was so nervous, we could barely hear her. Ms. Gonzalez nicely asked her to try to speak a little louder, but when she did, her voice shook. And she wouldn't even look at the class. I was very relieved when she didn't get any attitude from our classmates.

Alyssa was not as fortunate. When she got to the point where she said she'd decided not to run away from home, some boy muttered loudly, "I'll bet your parents wish you had." And got giggles. Also a very stern look from Ms. Gonzalez, but that was no comfort to Alyssa.

Only, Alyssa, being Alyssa, didn't need any comfort. She glared at the boy, fiercely, and he shrank back in his seat. Maybe he thought she was putting a curse on him.

After school, I waited outside for Alyssa and Rachel. Beyond the crowd of students pouring out of the building, lingering to talk or waiting for rides, I spotted Rachel's mom. Since Alyssa and I were going to Rachel's, I was about to head over in her direction when I heard my name.

I turned to find Mike Twersky standing there.

"Hey, Ellie."

My heartbeat went into overtime.

"Hi?" he said, and the question in his voice made me realize I hadn't said anything yet.

I came up with a snappy response. "Hi."

"You know Jim Berger?" he asked.

We'd never spoken, but I knew who he was—a short, skinny kid in my English class. I'd heard other boys tease him about this, but he ignored them.

I nodded.

"He's a friend of mine," Mike Twersky said.

Well, that was interesting. Cool guys weren't usually friends with people like Jim Berger. And I didn't know why he was telling me this.

He went on. "Jim told me about your report in class."

"Okay," I said, and even though I didn't think it was possible, my heartbeat quickened.

"About how your dad tried to start a homeless shelter in Brookdale and the whole town turned against him."

I nodded.

Then Mike nodded. "That's cool."

What, that the town practically threw us out? No, it couldn't be that. So I just said, "Really?"

"Yeah. My dad's on the town council. He volunteers at the Lakeside homeless shelter and my whole family volunteers at the soup kitchen on Sundays."

"Really?" I closed my eyes in despair. What was wrong with me? Had I completely lost my entire vocabulary?

He nodded.

And I repeated exactly what he'd said about *my* father. "That's—that's cool!"

"People shouldn't have to sleep on the streets," he said.

And all I could do was nod fervently and say again, "Really!"

Then we just stood there for a second in silence. But it was okay. We'd made a real connection.

"Well, see ya."

"See ya," I echoed.

I watched as he made his way through the crowd. An older girl glanced at me oddly as she walked by, and I realized I had a big stupid grin on my face.

Rachel emerged from the building, followed by Alyssa, and we joined Rachel's mom.

"I brought the car today," she told us. "I have to drop you all off and go on to a dentist's appointment. But it's okay," she assured us. "Cecilia's home grading papers this afternoon."

Like it would be so terrible if three girls our age stayed in a house alone in the middle of the afternoon. I wondered if Rachel still had to have a babysitter. Or maybe her parents never went out without her.

Rachel lived in a small, pretty house that looked like a beach cottage. It was all white on the outside, but the inside was full of color—sky-blue walls, colorful wall hangings, framed art posters, and lots of plants. Rachel's Mami greeted us warmly.

"Something to eat?" she asked us. I wasn't looking forward to that, since I envisioned a big bowl of celery sticks.

"Maybe later, Mami," Rachel said. "We've got work to do. I don't think Mom would mind if we use her computer."

"Is it for school?"

I mentally groaned as Rachel began to go pink in the face. The poor girl couldn't even bring herself to fib a little. And it wasn't even a fib—we were researching Kiara, and Kiara went to our school. So I jumped in and said a firm "Yes."

Rachel's mom had her graphic design office in a small study off the living room. Her computer had an enormous screen.

"Let me just adjust something," Rachel's Mami murmured, and she hit a few keys on her wife's computer. I had a feeling it was child protection software, so little Rachel wouldn't accidentally see something naughty. Fortunately, our kind of search didn't require the use of any words that would challenge the restrictions set up by the program.

She left us. Alyssa pulled out her laptop and I

pulled out mine, a hand-me-down from Charlotte. We got a couple of additional chairs from the dining room, connected to Rachel's Wi-Fi, and settled down in front of the big computer.

"I don't even know where we should start," Rachel said. "There have to be millions of games, right?"

"Hers is an RPG," I reported. "That narrows it."

"Not by much," Alyssa commented.

"You know about them?" I asked.

"Sure. Last year, I was really into a couple of them."

"What were they like?" I asked.

She smiled. "Oh, just your average dark, creepy, bloody games. With vampires." Then she looked serious. "But I got sick of them. The communities weren't fun. And some of them said really awful stuff to each other."

"Well, Kiara's game isn't one of those," I told them. "It's all cutesy animals."

I described what I'd seen in the media center, and Rachel went to work on the keyboard. She typed in search words: *role-play, animals* . . .

"What else?" she asked me.

"*Labyrinth. Maze.*"

Titles flew up on the screen. Also pictures.

Looking over Rachel's shoulder, I spotted one that resembled Kiara's game.

"Click on that."

Rachel did. *The Amazing Maze,*" she read aloud.

Lucky for us, it was a freebie.

"Okay, let's download it," Rachel said.

We did, and then each of us began reading the directions on our screens.

"Do you think we can just observe the game?" Rachel wondered aloud.

"It doesn't work like that, you can't just watch," Alyssa told us. "We have to join. So first we need to create our avatars."

This part was fun. We each had to choose an animal, name it, and customize its appearance. I picked a rabbit, made it blue with yellow stripes and red ears, and called myself FunnyBunny. Alyssa became a green-and-purple pig and named it PigglyWiggly. It took Rachel a while to choose, but she finally settled on a bear and colored it red.

"BigBadBear," she announced, but that was rejected since apparently another player was using that name. She had to add a number and became BigBadBear13.

"Now we're supposed to join a team," Alyssa said.

"We want to be on Kiara's team," I pointed out. "How do we do that?"

"The directions said you could join a friend's team if you know their screen name," said Rachel.

I closed my eyes, thinking back to when I'd watched Kiara playing in the media center. "SwanK," I told them. "With a capital letter *K*."

"Nice recall, FunnyBunny," Alyssa said.

We found SwanK, and we were in luck—she was online at that very moment! We added our screen names, and our avatars appeared at the entrance to the maze.

"I'm still not completely understanding how this works," Rachel murmured. Neither was I, and even Alyssa, the only one among us who'd ever played this sort of thing, was frowning at her screen.

"It says you should turn on the microphone," Rachel said.

"Don't do it!" Alyssa ordered.

"Why not?"

"I told you about the trash talking. It can get seriously nasty. And I'll bet these guys will be even worse than the vampires."

"Why?" I asked.

"They'll probably trash-talk with *animal* voices," Alyssa said darkly. "Do you really want to hear *that*?"

So none of us turned on our microphones.

We all entered the maze, but then things got really confusing. It seemed you could only move through the maze in certain directions and from particular spots, but we saw creatures from both teams whizzing from one spot to another without being able to figure out why or how.

Up in one corner of the screen was a scoreboard, where avatars in the maze were listed with points next to their names. Points rapidly increased and decreased, but none of us could understand the reasons points were added or subtracted.

"I still don't get it," Alyssa complained. "In the games I played, you just killed each other. Then, in one of them, the dead avatars turned into ghosts and you had to destroy them with special weapons."

"I don't see any weapons here," Rachel said. "The animals just seem to be shoving each other around."

I studied the action on my screen. "Okay, I think the points give an animal the right to shove another animal farther from the exit of the maze."

"No, I think they get the points *when* they shove," Alyssa said.

"Whatever," I said. "Either way, I think Kiara should just stay away from the animals with lots of points if she wants to get through this thing."

Alyssa pointed to the screen. "But that strategy's kind of impossible. The points change so fast that she'd have to be looking back and forth from the maze to the scoreboard really quickly. Like, a high-scoring animal probably could shove her away before she even knows he has the points to do it."

I was so confused. I hate games—or tests, or anything—with timers. I like to consider what I want to do, which is why I only play games where you aren't playing against anyone else and you can take as much time as you need to decide on your next move.

In the end we just watched SwanK. And after a while, it seemed like every time the swan was near an opening to pass through, another animal blocked her. FunkyMonkey and the others on her team never seemed to be anywhere near her. Then, as I watched the screen, SwanK was very close to advancing a good distance when she was suddenly swept back.

Alyssa was looking at the scoreboard. "Whoa—I think that was Ponygirl who sent her off! Her points just dropped."

"No way," I said. "Ponygirl is on her team. Why would she do that?"

"It must have been an accident," Rachel decided.

"Or maybe they don't really play as a team and each player is on their own."

Alyssa must have read the directions more closely than we did, because she was shaking her head vigorously. "No. If a team wins, with everyone through the maze before the other team, each member on the winning team gets the same number of points. But the highest-*ranking* person on the team gets three *times* as many points as everyone else, *and* gets to go into a final with the highest-ranking player on other teams."

We kept watching. SwanK got close to a gate that would let her move deeper inside the maze. But when she was only steps away, a crocodile blocked her.

"So...what should we do?" I asked.

"We're going to help her get out of the maze," Alyssa said with determination. "And destroy everyone who's in her way."

"That sounds violent," Rachel murmured.

"Just do what I tell you to do," Alyssa ordered her. "Get your bear behind the kangaroo. Ellie, you're in a position to block that chicken."

Not only did she operate her own pig, Alyssa called out the moves each of us should make on our screens. For an alienated lost soul, she was really getting into it. Our animals would block an opening to keep other animals from blocking it. Then, when Kiara's swan was very close, we'd move so she could get through.

"Do you think she's noticed we're helping her?" Rachel asked.

"Sure, if she's watching closely," Alyssa said. "Of course, she doesn't know that BigBadBear13 is you."

We got better and better, moving more and more quickly—all thanks to Alyssa. Rachel and I just followed her orders. And it worked—Kiara was first to get out of the maze!

"We saved her!" Alyssa crowed. And the three of us slapped hands in victory.

On the screen, the name SwanK lit up in gold with stars all around the swan. And on the message board, there was a message for us: "FunnyBunny, PigglyWiggly, BigBadBear13, thank you! And welcome to the team!"

We cheered and gave each other high fives.

"We're her friends now!" I declared.

"Only in the game," Alyssa reminded me.

"But once she knows who we are, she'll like us," Rachel said happily.

Our screens flashed with a NEW GAME sign.

"Want to play another game?" Alyssa asked. "I could get into this."

"Rachel!" came a voice from another room.

"¿Sí, Mami?"

"¿Tienen hambre ahora, chicas?"

Alyssa and I looked at Rachel.

"She wants to know if we're hungry," Rachel said.

I was suddenly aware that my stomach had been growling for some time now.

We were all ready for snacks, so we followed Rachel into the dining room. I'd prepared myself for carrot sticks, but Rachel's Mami had put out a very nice spread for us. There was a cucumber salad with mint and sour cream, pita bread, enormous oatmeal cookies that were positively yummy, and a fancy fruit drink made with mangos and kiwis.

"¡Espero que estén contentas con esto!"

"Gracias, Mami, se ve delicioso," Rachel said.

Rachel's mother blew her a kiss, beamed at all of us, and left the room.

Alyssa turned to Rachel. "You speak Spanish." As usual, being Alyssa, she made it sound almost like an accusation.

"I told you, Mami's from Mexico. Mom speaks Spanish too. Sometimes we speak in English, sometimes in Spanish, sometimes both at the same time." She laughed. "Sometimes Mami thinks everyone can understand Spanish."

"Have you ever been to Mexico?" I asked.

"Sure. We usually go at Christmas to see my abuela."

"Your what?"

Rachel grinned. "My grandmother. Abuela."

Alyssa cocked her head thoughtfully. "It's prettier in Spanish."

"Hey, we can sign up for a language class next year," I remarked. "Maybe Alyssa and I should take Spanish. Then you can help us if we have a hard time with it."

"Good idea," Alyssa said, helping herself to another cookie.

And Rachel nodded in approval.

I suddenly felt super good. When we left Brookdale, I'd told myself I never wanted any friends again. But how could I live without these good feelings? *Kiara needs this,* I thought. Avatars could never substitute for real friends.

Out of the blue, Alyssa suddenly turned to me and said, "So. I saw you talking to Mike Twersky this afternoon." Once again, her statement sounded like an accusation.

Back in Brookdale, if one of my friends liked a boy, she talked about him. I remembered countless lunch-table and sleepover conversations about crushes and fantasies. But I couldn't do that here, not with my new friends. We'd bonded as loners, outcasts. If I admitted to feelings for a popular boy, this would be like a betrayal. He was one of "them."

Alyssa was waiting for a response, and Rachel was looking at me curiously too.

I came up with an excuse. "Yeah. He's in my pre-algebra class and he forgot to write down the homework."

That seemed to satisfy them, though I could have sworn I saw a hint of suspicion in Alyssa's eyes. I was uncomfortable. Not just with Alyssa's expression, but with the fact that I wasn't sharing something with my friends. I looked out the window.

"It's getting late. I should get home."

Rachel's Mami came into the dining room just as I said that.

"Is a parent coming to pick you up?" she asked me.

"No, but it's okay, I can walk."

She looked concerned. "Maybe Alyssa's parent can drop you off."

"No, they're both still at work," Alyssa said. "I'm walking too."

"It's not far for them, Mami," Rachel said.

"But it's almost dark out," her mother protested. "I'll drive you."

Just then, Rachel sneezed.

"Oh, Rachel. That cold's not coming back, is it?" She reached out to feel Rachel's forehead.

"It's nothing, Mami, I feel fine."

"Well, I don't want you going outside." Her brow furrowed. "And you can't stay home alone while I take your friends."

"But you don't need to," I told her. "It's only five o'clock. I walk by myself after the sun goes down, if it's not too late."

"So do I," Alyssa said. "Most kids our age can do that."

I couldn't believe she said that, right to Rachel's mother's face. And then I looked at Rachel. She was nodding!

"She's right, Mami. They're not babies. I'm not a baby."

I was surprised. Was Rachel actually protesting?

But we were spared any battles because just then Rachel's mom returned home, to her Mami's obvious relief.

"Hey, how was the dentist, Mom?" Rachel called.

"He was pretty gentle, hon," her mom said as she

unwound her scarf. "And the good news is that the filling's fixed and I won't have that painful toothache anymore."

"So you feel okay?" asked Rachel's Mami, giving her wife a sympathetic hug. "I want to drive Alyssa and Ellie home, but I didn't want Rachel to go outside. I'm wondering if her cold is still hanging on."

Immediately, Rachel's mom looked alarmed. "I'll get the thermometer."

"Mom, I don't have a fever, I feel fine!"

Alyssa and I quickly said our goodbyes and thank-yous and left with Rachel's Mami. She dropped me off first. "Are you going to be alone in the house?" she asked worriedly. "Aren't both your parents working?"

"Yes, but my father works in his home office," I assured her. I didn't actually know for sure if he was there at that moment—sometimes he went out for meetings. It didn't matter, I had my own key. But I could just imagine Cecilia Levin-Lopez insisting on staying here till she was sure someone was in the house.

Alyssa would have to go through the same interrogation when they got to her place, I thought. Maybe the fact that she had older siblings—*step*siblings— would satisfy Rachel's mother.

Dad *was* home, and he wasn't in a meeting. He came out of his office when he heard me walk in.

"Oh, good, you're home," he said happily. "You can help me make a cake."

I was puzzled. It wasn't anyone's birthday. "What's the occasion?"

"Your mother's first day at her new job!"

I'd totally forgotten. And I felt very guilty. I knew this was a big deal for her. As I followed Dad to the kitchen, I thought about how I never paid much attention to what was going on in my parents' lives. Unless it affected me, of course. Like, back in Brookdale, when we were all shunned because of the homeless shelter plan—I never thought about how *they* were feeling.

Even in that report I'd given this morning in English—I only talked about how *I* had suffered. And then I remembered the pride in Mike Twersky's voice when he talked about *his* father.

I must have looked troubled, because Dad asked, "Is everything okay, honey?"

"Oh, sure," I said.

He started pulling cake-making stuff out of cabinets. "Are you feeling better about Lakeside now?"

"Yeah." I opened the refrigerator and took out

butter and eggs. "Dad...what you did back in Brookdale—"

"I know," he interrupted. "It was hard on you."

"Yes. But it was the right thing. *You* did the right thing," I said. "Trying to give people shelter. That was important. I don't know why people were so mean about it."

"NIMBY," he said simply.

"Huh?"

"'Not in my backyard.' People might think a homeless shelter is a good idea in the abstract, but not when it's nearby. Not when it might affect them personally."

"But it has to be somewhere," I said. I took a deep breath and met his eyes. "I'm sorry I made such a fuss about moving."

He gazed back at me, just a little sadly. "You don't blame me for disrupting your life?"

Maybe I did, then. But not anymore. "You did the right thing," I repeated. "I'm proud of you, Daddy."

I hadn't called him Daddy for a long time, not since I was little. I could tell he liked it.

"Thank you, honey." He kissed the top of my head. "Now start beating those eggs."

eleven

I WOKE UP FEELING GOOD THE NEXT MORNING.

When Mom came home the night before, she was in a great mood. She regaled us with tales of her new job, the people she'd met, the stories she was going to take on. And she gushed over the cake Dad and I had made to celebrate.

Just like my father, my mother was happy to be here in Lakeside. And I was getting into that mind-set too. Back in Brookdale, before all the drama, I'd thought I was happy. I was comfortable in my clique, I wasn't bullied or laughed at, and all was well.

But it wasn't all that interesting. Every day was the same, and it seemed like my friends and I were always talking about the same things. With Alyssa and Rachel, I was having adventures. I didn't even think of my new friends as weird anymore. They were special. And with them, I felt special too.

Before leaving the house that morning, I took a quick detour to the turret. Scanning the town, I spotted Kiara-the-swan on the banks of a fake lake. With her were a blue-and-yellow-striped rabbit with red ears, a green-and-purple pig, and a red bear, and they all seemed to be playing together. I couldn't wait to tell Alyssa and Rachel!

I connected with them just before English class and announced my news.

"Wow. So...does that mean we're her friends now?" Rachel asked.

I nodded. "Well, FunnyBunny, PigglyWiggly, and BigBadBear13 are her friends. But like Alyssa said, she doesn't know they're us."

We could see Kiara herself approaching the door. Alyssa spoke in a whisper. "Should we tell her now?"

"Let's wait till lunch," I said. "We'll have more time to explain and really bond together."

Lunchtime couldn't come fast enough for me.

I had it all worked out in my head—Kiara's surprise when she learned who had saved her in the game. Her whole new attitude toward us. We'd tell her about the spyglass, and I'd invite her to join us that afternoon in the turret.

In the cafeteria, Rachel waited with her lunch bag while Alyssa and I went through the line. Then we headed over to the table where Kiara sat alone, as usual.

She looked up and frowned.

"Okay if we sit with you?" I asked.

"Why?" she asked. Her tone was totally unfriendly, but that didn't bother me. I knew this would change very soon.

"We've got something to tell you," I said. I'd already decided that I was going to take on the leadership role in this conversation. Alyssa could be too aggressive, and Rachel was too shy.

Kiara didn't respond, and she was still frowning. But I sat down anyway and Rachel and Alyssa took the chairs next to me.

Kiara returned to her food and didn't even ask what we wanted to tell her. So I jumped in.

"It's about *The Amazing Maze.*"

Kiara put her fork down and made eye contact. Those eyes were narrow.

"I *told* you to stop spying on me!"

"I wasn't spying, I was playing. All of us were."

She still looked suspicious, so I explained.

"Remember yesterday, when you were stuck in the maze? And three players helped you out?"

Could those eyes *get* any narrower? She was practically squinting. I went on.

"Well, Kiara, please allow me to introduce myself. I'm FunnyBunny." I looked at Alyssa, and she spoke.

"I'm PigglyWiggly."

And then Rachel softly piped up. "I'm BigBad-Bear13."

Kiara's eyes went from squints to saucers. I waited for a great big smile.

It didn't come.

"You shouldn't have intruded on my game," she declared. "That was inappropriate."

Alyssa broke in, and as I'd feared, she went hostile. "Hey, you don't own it, anyone can play. You can't keep us out."

"We're on your team now, Kiara" I said. "We could all play together."

"But, you didn't ask me if that's what *I* wanted" Kiara said in a matter-of-fact tone. "I didn't invite you to join my game. Or sit at my table. Please leave me alone."

Now I was absolutely, positively stunned. Rachel looked like she was about to burst into tears. Alyssa stood up and snapped something that would have sent her to the office if a teacher had heard her

Rachel whispered, "I'm sorry." She and I both got up, and the three of us went to another table.

"I don't get it," Rachel said mournfully. "Why does she hate us?"

"She hates everybody," Alyssa declared. "I mean, really. I don't know why we bothered. Have you ever seen her with other people?"

I didn't remind her that I'd never seen her and Rachel with other people either until we came together.

"I say we just forget her," Alyssa continued.

I frowned. "I don't know. I just think maybe she belongs with the Spyglass Sisterhood."

At the same time, Alyssa and Rachel said, "The what?"

I honestly didn't know why I'd said that—it just slipped out. But it sounded right.

"That's us, that's our name. We're the Spyglass Sisterhood. What do you think?"

"I like it!" Rachel exclaimed.

Alyssa shrugged. "Guess it's okay." But she liked it too, I could tell.

"And you really think Kiara would fit in, after what just happened?" Rachel asked.

"I just have a feeling about her," I said. "Like, maybe she's not really mean or stuck up. She wasn't calling us names or yelling at us or anything back there. She was just…saying what happened. We thought she'd be okay with what we did, but she wasn't."

"So?" said Alyssa.

"So, I don't think she hates us. Maybe it's something else. Maybe she's embarrassed. Or maybe she's sad."

Rachel dug into her quinoa salad and chewed thoughtfully. "You said she lives with her dad, right? That's sort of unusual, if her parents are divorced."

"Maybe her mom didn't want custody," Alyssa said. "That would make a person sad."

"Or maybe her mom passed away," I added. "That would make her even sadder. I wonder how we can find out?"

"We could search for her online," Alyssa suggested. "If her mother died, there would be an obituary."

"Hey, we've got internet now," I told them. "Why don't you guys come over after school? We could do some searching for Kiara *and* look in the spyglass."

After lunch, I had pre-algebra. When I reached the classroom, I saw Mike Twersky standing outside the door. My heart automatically started to flutter.

He glanced up as I approached. He wasn't actually looking at me, but he said "Hi."

"Hi," I replied.

He still wasn't looking at me, but he spoke again. "I wanted to ask you something."

The fluttering increased. He was waiting for *me*!

He still wasn't making good eye contact, but that didn't bother me. From my limited experiences with boys, I knew they weren't always comfortable looking a girl in the eyes. I didn't know why—maybe someday I'd know a boy well enough to ask. But for now, I just waited patiently to find out what he wanted.

"Um, you said I could come over sometime and look through your telescope."

He paused, so I interjected an encouraging "Yeah."

"So...I was wondering if I could come over after school today. If that's okay."

My heart sank. I'd just told Alyssa and Rachel to come over. "Maybe later? Like, after dinner?"

He shook his head. "Well...it'll be dark by then."

I felt like an idiot. Of course you couldn't see birds in the dark. And I couldn't give up this opportunity.

"Actually, it's okay. After school."

"You sure?" he asked. "You don't have something else to do?"

"Uh, well, I thought I did, but...I don't. So, yes. You can definitely come over after school."

He smiled. *That* practically took my breath away. "Great."

"I'll give you my address."

"Why don't we just meet after the last class and go together?" he suggested.

Now my head started to spin.

It wasn't that I didn't consider myself worthy to be seen in public with a cute guy like Mike Twersky. I might not have been one of the cool girls here, but I *did* have self-esteem.

But I'd already observed that here at East Lakeside, the rules of boy-and-girl-together were the same as they'd been back at Brookdale. Boys and girls didn't sit together in the cafeteria, or walk together in the halls, and I hadn't noticed any couples hanging out together outside after school.

So apparently, Mike didn't observe the traditional middle school social regulations. I liked that.

I managed to catch up with Rachel in the hall between classes, and I told her about the change in plans. Her already big eyes went huge.

"You've got a boyfriend!" she squealed.

"Shh!" I lowered my own voice. "No, it's not like that." I grinned. "But…yeah. He's nice."

Rachel hugged herself in glee. "Call me tonight and tell me everything!"

I wasn't able to find Alyssa until after school, when I ran out of my last class and cornered her at her locker. I explained hurriedly.

"Listen, I can't meet with you guys today. Mike Twersky wants to come over and look in the spyglass."

Alyssa's eyebrows shot up. "You're inviting Mike Twersky to join the Spyglass Sisterhood?"

I shook my head. "No. He thinks it's an ordinary telescope. He just wants to look at . . at stuff." I didn't know if maybe his bird watching was some sort of secret, since it wasn't exactly like shooting hoops or whatever.

Now Alyssa's expression went stone cold. "So you're blowing us off to get into the popular crowd?"

"No! That has nothing to do with it. It's that—I like him. Kind of. You know what I mean."

"No, Ellie. I don't." With that, she slammed her locker shut and stormed away.

I stared after her in shock. Was she really angry? I was upset, but I couldn't stand here and think about it. And I couldn't run after her. I had to meet Mike.

It was funny, how I now felt comfortable thinking of him as Mike, not Mike Twersky. Like we were actually friends. As I walked quickly to the exit, I tried to imagine what we might talk about as we walked together. Birds? Or maybe just the usual stuff kids who didn't know each other very well talked about. Complaints about homework, teachers we didn't like, the crummy food in the cafeteria, that sort of thing.

He was waiting just outside the door. We exchanged the usual greetings and started walking through the parking lot. At one point, we passed Paige with some of her friends, and they were all looking at us with very surprised expressions. I had to admit to myself that felt kind of good. A couple of them called, "Hi, Mike," and he waved in response. Of course, they didn't say, "Hi, Ellie." And I didn't care at all—which also felt good.

And I didn't have to start a conversation—because *he* did!

"So how do you like Lakeside?" he asked.

I wasn't sure if he meant the school or the town, so I gave a general response. "It's nice."

"They're going to build a really cool community center over there," he said, pointing.

"I know," I replied, and almost blurted out that I'd seen it, but I caught myself in time. "My dad told me about it."

"Yeah, my dad's been talking about it too. He wants to know if the folks in the homeless shelter will be able to use it."

"Why wouldn't they?" I asked.

"Well, it's supposed to be only for residents of Lakeside, and some people don't think the shelter is a real residence. *I* think they're just afraid of people who aren't exactly like they are."

"That's not cool," I remarked. "I like knowing people who are nothing like me."

"Yeah, I can tell. I've seen you with that girl who wears black all the time."

"Alyssa. She was my first friend here." Although after our last encounter, I wasn't so sure we were *still* friends. I pushed that worrisome thought to the back of my mind.

"My dad says he might have to see a lawyer, to make sure the shelter residents can get into the community center."

"My dad's a lawyer."

"Really? Cool. I'll tell my dad."

I couldn't believe it—we were having a real conversation about real stuff. It lasted all the way to my house.

When we went inside, I could see that my dad's office door was closed, which meant he was meeting with a client. Which was just as well—Mike's and my relationship hadn't reached the "meet the parents" point yet. If it even *was* a relationship.

I took his coat, took mine off, and put them both on the coatrack by the door. Our coats, together. Side by side. Then I led Mike up to the turret.

"Wow, that's a really old telescope," he commented. It wasn't a criticism—he was looking at it in admiration.

"It works pretty well," I told him. "And you can magnify what you see." I demonstrated the dial. "Go ahead, try it."

I waited in suspense as he peered through the eyepiece. What would he see? Would the spyglass reveal something to him? And if it did, should I tell him about the Spyglass Sisterhood? Would he want to join? We'd have to change the name, then. Spyglass Peoplehood? That didn't sound as good.

He let out a whoop. I held my breath. But I had nothing to worry about.

"A white-breasted nuthatch! I can see the cap!" He turned to me. "Take a look."

I saw a bird.

"Does the cap look black to you?" he asked. "If it's gray, it's female."

"It looks more like a very, very dark gray. But that could be the sun."

Mike pulled a book from his backpack. "Remember that book I took out of the library? I bought a paperback copy so I could check off birds I've seen. Is the nuthatch still in the tree?"

"Yeah."

Quickly, he flipped some pages, looked at a picture, and asked me to step aside. I did.

"No, definitely a male. If it was a female, it would be a lighter gray. Oops, there he goes."

He made a mark in his book and looked very pleased with himself.

"Why don't you let me hold the book?" I suggested. "You can call out what you see, I'll look it up, and then you can compare the picture with the bird right away."

"Great idea." He handed me the book.

He called out the birds he saw: a wren, a gull, and a white-winged crossbill. None stuck around long enough for me to see them, but that was okay because they would all probably look the same to me from a distance. I found them in the book and checked them off. At one point, it occurred to me that maybe the spyglass was showing him the birds he wanted to see. But of course, I couldn't tell him that.

"Red-tailed hawk!"

"Got it!"

"We make a good team," he said.

I couldn't remember any boy ever speaking to me like that before. I couldn't even respond. I just smiled and nodded happily.

Then the sun began to set, and soon nothing else could be spotted. He took the book back from me and put it in his backpack.

"You're really into bird watching," I said.

"Yeah. I guess it's my number one hobby."

"Do your friends watch birds too?"

He shook his head. "Nah, I've told them about it but they're not interested. I'm thinking maybe I should join a club or something, so I can have other people to talk about birds."

I tried to sound casual, offhand. "I think it's interesting. I'd like to know more about it."

"Yeah?"

"Yeah."

There was a moment of silence. "Want something to eat?" I asked.

"Thanks, but I can't, I have to get home. It's my night to help make dinner."

"You can cook?"

He grinned. "I can slice and chop, that's about it. But I have two younger brothers and a sister, so there's always a lot of slicing and chopping to do."

I went downstairs with him and gave him his coat.

"That was great," he said. "I don't know if I could have seen those birds with my binoculars. You can cover a wider area with a telescope."

"You can come again," I said. "Anytime you want."

"Thanks."

I opened the door, and he started out. But then he paused and looked back at me. "I mean it, really. Thanks a lot. That was fun."

I nodded. "Yes, it was."

Then he was gone. I shut the door, leaned against it, and closed my eyes.

"Ellie? Are you okay?"

I hadn't even heard my father come out of his office.

"I'm fine," I said quickly. "Just—just thinking about all the homework I have to do."

"But you're smiling."

"Well, it's...it's interesting homework." I fled up the stairs.

I *did* have a lot of homework, and I'd left my backpack in the turret. Up there, I couldn't resist a quick look through the spyglass. Maybe I could see a future vision of Mike and me, strolling along, holding hands...

It wasn't dusk out there anymore. It was daytime, but very cloudy, and a light rain was falling. The spyglass was showing me the kind of day that could make a person feel unhappy, only nothing could really get me down at that moment.

But I did see something that cut into my joy. On the lake that wasn't really there, a swan floated. All alone—no FunnyBunny, no PigglyWiggly, no Big-BadBear13. And none of the other creatures I'd seen her playing with either.

It was just SwanK, by herself. No friends. And even though I couldn't see any expression on her face, I just knew that Kiara was sad.

I wasn't going to give up. I had to reach her.

twelve

ON FRIDAY MORNING, AS I WALKED TO SCHOOL, I was thinking about Mike. As I walked to my locker, I thought about Kiara. But as I made my way to English class, the only person in my head was Alyssa. And when I saw her, wearing a stony glare, waiting outside the classroom door with Rachel, I didn't know what to expect from her.

Certainly not the first words that came out of her mouth.

"I've decided to forgive you."

I was so surprised, I couldn't think of anything to say. Fortunately, Alyssa continued.

"I shouldn't have been so angry. But you see, I have trust issues."

I spoke carefully. "I'm not exactly sure what that means."

"I never think I can count on people. Like, I'm sure they'll always let me down."

I was still a little confused, but I managed an "Okay."

"It's a typical attitude of the social outcast," Alyssa explained. "We just don't trust other people. Unless they're also outcasts, of course."

"Well, I'm sorry I had to change our plans yesterday," I told her.

Rachel stepped into the conversation. "Only, you didn't *have* to," she said. "You *wanted* to."

That *really* surprised me. I'd never heard Rachel make a critical statement like that. And she was reprimanding me!

She was right, of course. I didn't *have* to break our plans. It wasn't like I was feeling sick or being kept after school for detention. It was my choice.

"I'm sorry," I said again, but more humbly this time. Because it truly wasn't nice of me, what I'd done. Then I looked at Rachel curiously. "But...you weren't angry at me, the way Alyssa was."

"I guess that's because I don't have trust issues," Rachel replied. "And because you and Alyssa... well, you're like my first real friends. You guys accept me. I didn't want to lose that by getting into an argument."

I thought about this. "I guess I don't have trust issues either. Because I trusted that you two would still be my friends. And you'd forgive me, because that's what friends do. And you'd understand, because I've got a serious crush on this guy, and—"

Alyssa broke in. "Okay, okay, we get it, we're still friends. Here comes Ms. Gonzalez."

We hurried into the classroom just as the bell started to ring. As I passed Kiara to take my seat behind hers, I said, "Hi." I didn't expect her to respond. And she didn't.

"I still don't know how we're going to get through to her," I told the others later at lunch. "She won't even *look* at me."

"We *were* going to Google her family," Rachel reminded me. "See if we can find anything out about them."

"Right. Yeah, let's do that at my place after school," I said.

"What if Mike Twersky wants to come over?" Alyssa asked.

I replied firmly. "I'll tell him he can't, that I'm busy today."

I didn't get the opportunity to keep my promise. In pre-algebra, Mike was hanging with some guys when I walked in, and when class was over, he stayed to speak to the teacher. So after school, I met the girls, and we went to my house.

We started off searching the name Kiara Douglas. And there were several of them, all over the country. When we clicked on them, a few were total dead ends, and the few we could get *some* info about were clearly wrong—too young or too old. She wasn't on Facebook, she didn't have an Instagram account.

We found her father's name in the school directory, but Googling him only told us that he was a professor at Bascomb College. We couldn't Google her mother for an obituary or anything because we didn't know her first name.

"We're not getting anywhere," said Alyssa, sitting back and sounding annoyed.

"Okay. What's everything we know about Kiara?" Rachel asked.

"We know she spends her time alone, that she doesn't have any friends, and that she claims to not want any," I said.

"What we don't know is why," said Rachel.

"Let's check the spyglass," I suggested. "Maybe it will show us something new."

Up in the turret, we took turns scanning the town, but the spyglass didn't reveal anything—no Kiara or SwanK, and nothing interesting about anyone else either. Not even Mr. Clark, dancing with Ms. Hannigan. Alyssa was getting impatient and Rachel looked a little depressed. I felt bad, helpless, as if I'd personally disappointed them.

Rachel seemed to sense my feelings. "It's not your fault, Ellie."

"Maybe it's broken," Alyssa said, and slapped the side of the telescope.

I flinched. "I don't think so. I *hope* not." I really meant that too. A broken spyglass would mean no more Spyglass Sisterhood.

"Maybe it just needs a break," Rachel suggested. "We've been working it pretty hard."

Alyssa frowned. "You're making it sound like it's

human. *Things* don't get tired." Then she cocked her head thoughtfully. "Unless it needs a battery."

"It doesn't run on batteries," I said.

"It's magic," Rachel pointed out. "Maybe it makes its own rules."

We all just stood there, staring at it. Finally, I said, "Want some food?"

But just then we heard a strange tinkling sound. Rachel looked at the spyglass hopefully, but Alyssa began fumbling in her bag.

"It's my phone," she muttered. She took it out, looked at the screen, and made a face. But she accepted the call.

"Hi, Mom."

After a few seconds, she groaned. "Can't Josh or Madison do it?"

She listened and grimaced. Whatever she was hearing couldn't be good news.

"Okay, okay, I'll go. Bye." She tossed the phone back in her bag.

"What's up?" I asked.

"My mom's been called in to do some emergency surgery, so I have to pick up my little brother at the playhouse. His rehearsal's running long and she doesn't want him going home alone after dark."

"She sounds like my mothers," Rachel said.

"There's a big difference," Alyssa pointed out. "Ethan's nine and you're almost thirteen."

I thought that sounded kind of mean, but Rachel didn't seem to be insulted. She just sighed and said, "Yeah, I know."

"You guys want to come with me?" Alyssa asked.

I didn't have any urgent homework to do—tomorrow was Saturday. And I was curious to know more about Alyssa's family. Rachel nodded too.

"Isn't one of your parents coming to pick you up here?" I asked.

Rachel did a not-so-bad imitation of an Alyssa shrug. "I'll call them. I'll tell them I'm going to do something with you guys and I'll get myself home."

I looked at her with interest. Was Rachel declaring independence? Was a rebellion in the works?

"Tell them we'll walk you home," Alyssa said. "No point in making them hysterical."

Now, *that* was interesting too. Alyssa, showing concern for parents? Was everyone behaving differently today except me? Maybe there was something in the air. Maybe, on Monday, Kiara Douglas would be friendly. But I doubted it.

Rachel made her call, I left a note for my parents, and we collected our coats. I remembered passing the playhouse once, and it wasn't near here.

"How are we getting there? Bus?"

Alyssa waved her cell phone. "I get to use a ride-share app when I have to do a family errand." She tapped on her phone, waited a few seconds, and then announced, "The driver will be here in three minutes." Then she turned to me.

"Okay, what's Mike Twersky really like?"

"He's nice," I replied.

Alyssa shook her head. "I have never known a popular kid who was nice."

"He's not like them," I told her.

"How is he different?"

I tried to think of a good example. "The other day, he stopped a guy at his table from tripping a smaller kid in the cafeteria. The big guy is named Thayer something."

Alyssa shuddered. "I know Thayer. He's a bully. Mike Twersky's friends with him?"

"Probably not close friends. I mean, he's friends with Jim Berger too. He's not a bully."

Alyssa still looked dubious.

"He's also into bird watching," I added. I hadn't told her that before, but at this point I figured if anything was going to convince her Mike was different, now would be the time to share it.

That statement reduced Alyssa to momentary silence.

"Really?"

"Yep. That's why he wanted to look in the spyglass. He didn't see anything except birds," I added. "And I didn't tell him about the Spyglass Sisterhood."

They both looked relieved. It was still our secret.

"I wonder if we'll ever see anything again," Rachel said wistfully.

At that moment, our car arrived. We didn't say much during the ride, probably because we were thinking about the spyglass and couldn't let the driver hear us.

We arrived at the Lakeside Playhouse, and Alyssa led us to the stage door on the side of the building. We followed her down a corridor lined with doors.

"Dressing rooms," Alyssa said, pointing at doors as we walked. "Props. Sets. Wardrobe." Clearly, she knew a lot about her little brother's theater world. I wondered if she was really as alienated from her family as she claimed to be.

"You've been here before," I said.

"Well, sure. Someone has to do the dirty work in the family."

We'd started hearing voices, and I realized we

were approaching the rehearsal. A man standing by the curtain put a finger to his lips.

There were three actors on the stage—a man, a woman, and a little boy who I presumed was Alyssa's brother. A voice coming from someone I couldn't see rang out.

"No, no! Laura, you're supposed to be off-book by now! And George, you should have moved stage left! Take five. Then we're going to go through this scene again."

Alyssa translated for them. "*Off-book* means the lines are memorized. *Take five* means a five-minute break."

The cute little kid with silky black hair waved to Alyssa and ambled toward us. I couldn't resist a glance at Alyssa's expression. She was actually smiling a real smile, not a smirk. Of course, being Alyssa, she didn't bother to introduce us. Her brother, however, was more well-behaved.

"Hi, I'm Ethan. Are you Alyssa's friends?"

There was something about the way he asked this that made me think he'd never met any friends of Alyssa's before. Rachel and I told him our names and assured him that yes, we were his sister's friends. He seemed very happy to hear it.

When he had to go back onstage for the rehearsal,

Alyssa considered what we should do while we waited.

"Oh, I know, let's look at the costumes," she said, and she took us to the door labeled WARDROBE.

The large room was packed with freestanding racks of clothes. A young woman sat at a table, running some fabric through a sewing machine. She looked up with a frown as we entered, but then she offered a small smile.

"Hi, Alyssa."

"Hi," Alyssa replied. "Okay if we look around?"

"Sure." To us, she said, "I'm Carrie Dale, the wardrobe mistress." She looked pointedly at Alyssa as she spoke.

Alyssa sighed. "Sorry," she said, and introduced us. And now Alyssa was being polite! How many more shocking experiences would I have today?

"Are you making a costume?" Rachel asked Ms. Dale.

"No, just fixing a seam. Feel free to explore, but tell me if you take anything off a rack. It may not look like it, but everything's organized."

There were some amazing clothes on the racks—long dresses with hoopskirts that looked like they would suit a woman from a hundred and fifty years ago. A man's tuxedo, a child's pinafore, gowns covered in sequins. Shelves on the walls held hats, masks, jewelry. I saw costumes that were immediately identifiable—pirates, princesses, clowns—and others that weren't, like a long yellow tube and a big purple ball of fur.

"Wow," I said. "They must put on a lot of plays."

"When I was younger, Mom and Mami took me to the children's plays they perform on Saturday afternoons," Rachel told us.

"The playhouse is a big deal," Alyssa explained. "It's known even outside Lakeside. Important people come here to scout out new talent. That's how Ethan got his commercial jobs."

"Hey, check this out!" Rachel exclaimed. "Ms. Dale, can I take this off the shelf?"

The wardrobe mistress looked up from her machine. "Okay."

I turned to see what Rachel had found. She was holding what looked like a headband with two big floppy ears attached.

"Bow your chin," she ordered me. Carefully she placed the band on my head, and I discovered that a transparent plastic wire holding a pink blob was dangling from it. Rachel fixed the blob onto my nose.

"Look, Alyssa!" she called. "It's FunnyBunny!"

Alyssa started laughing. I went to the big

full-length mirror on one wall and examined myself. I was about to laugh when an amazing thought came to me.

Watching my expression, Rachel asked, "What's the matter?"

"I just had an idea." I went to Ms. Dale.

"Do you have a pig mask?" I asked her.

"We have three pig heads," she told me. "We do *Three Little Pigs* every year."

She pointed me toward a cabinet on the other side of the room. Alyssa and Rachel followed me there. Opening it, I saw a bunch of heads—an alligator (or maybe it was a crocodile), monsters, assorted creatures I couldn't identify. And three pigs.

I pulled one out. Alyssa lowered her head, and I put it on her.

"Can you see?" I asked.

"Yeah, there are holes in the eyes. And the nose."

I searched the cabinet for something else but didn't see it. I hurried back to Ms. Dale.

"What about a bear?"

"There are whole costumes for bears. *Goldilocks,* rack eight."

Sure enough, there were three brown fuzzy jumpsuits in different sizes, all with attached headpieces. I picked out the smallest. "Rachel, try this on!"

It was a little too tight. Mama Bear was better, but the legs were too long.

"Just hold them up," I advised her.

We went to the mirror, Rachel hobbling as she tried to walk in the too-big costume.

"Now, look at us together," I ordered. "Funny-Bunny, PigglyWiggly, and BigBadBear."

"Thirteen," Rachel mumbled. Apparently, the mouth opening on the face of the costume didn't match her actual mouth.

"Right, BigBadBear13. What do you think?"

"*The Amazing Maze!*" Alyssa exclaimed. And through her thick fur face, Rachel made an excited sound. Clearly, I didn't have to tell them my idea.

The wardrobe mistress joined us. "I'll bet you want me to take a picture for Instagram, right?"

"Well, no, actually, I was wondering...could we borrow these? Just for tonight?"

Ms. Dale shook her head. "I'm sorry, girls, but we have a very strict rule about costumes. Nothing leaves the theater."

I couldn't see Alyssa's or Rachel's face, but I knew they had to be just as disappointed as I was.

Just then, the door opened, and a man walked in.

"What's going on?" he asked sharply.

I recognized his voice—he was the director of the play in rehearsal.

Alyssa strode toward him. "Mr. Kelly, can we borrow these costumes? And bring them back tomorrow?"

The look on the man's face told me the answer would be no. But before he could say it, Alyssa pulled off the pig head. His expression immediately softened.

"Oh. You're Ethan's sister."

She nodded. "Alyssa Parker."

He hesitated. "I assume you need them for some kind of costume party? You'll have to be very careful, don't tear them or spill anything on them."

"We'll be careful," Alyssa said.

Mr. Kelly didn't look thrilled, but he nodded at Ms. Dale and left the room.

As we moved away from the mirror, Rachel forgot to lift the trousers and tripped. She struggled back upright, and we checked to make sure the costume wasn't damaged. Rachel wasn't damaged either, but I worried that this could be a problem.

Alyssa went to Ms. Dale and asked to borrow some pins. She returned with them, and she and I knelt down on the floor to pin up Rachel's legs.

"I can't believe he said yes," I said to Alyssa. "He must really like you."

"No, he thinks I'm weird, like everyone else. It's because of my parents. They're patrons. They give a ton of money to the theater. He probably thinks they gave me permission to ask for the costumes. Okay, Rachel, is that better?"

Rachel took a few tentative steps and nodded.

"Then let's get my brother and go."

"Like this?" I asked.

Alyssa secured a paper bag from the wardrobe mistress, and we took off our masks and helped Rachel out of her costume so she wouldn't get stuck with any pins. Then we went to collect Ethan.

Alyssa was just about to call the rideshare service when Mr. Kelly came toward us.

"Would you and Ethan like a ride home?" he asked.

"Sure. Thanks. But actually, it's all of us. Is that okay?"

Again, he didn't look too thrilled, but clearly he would do anything to make the Parker family happy. So we all piled in with our costume bag and the director drove us to Alyssa's.

I'd only seen her house from the outside before. Inside, it was just as modern, with lots of chrome and glass and open spaces. When we walked in, we saw a very handsome teenage boy sprawled on the floor in front of what looked like an elaborate sound system. He took off the headset and looked at us.

I assumed this was Josh, the stepbrother, but of course Alyssa didn't bother to introduce us.

"Are the parents home?" she asked anxiously.

"No, not yet."

She looked relieved. "Can you feed Ethan?" she asked, making the statement sound more like an order than a question.

"Sure," he said.

Ethan joined him, and they left the room together.

"Wait here," Alyssa instructed us.

She returned with a pamphlet in her hand and held it up to show us.

"*The East Lakeside Middle School Student Directory,*" I read aloud.

"Here she is," Alyssa said, and pointed to the entry for Kiara Douglas. "And it's within walking distance!"

But it wasn't *that* close, the sun had gone down, and this felt like the coldest evening ever. Even in our puffy coats, mittens, and hats, we were freezing by the time we reached Kiara's street. We watched the numbers on the houses and came to the elegant apartment building I'd seen through the telescope.

"This is it," Alyssa said. But when we got to the door, we found we couldn't open it. There was a plaque on the side of the door with numbers next to buttons. It was one of those places where the person you were visiting had to know who you were and buzz you in.

"Does her address give the apartment number?" I asked.

Alyssa checked in the school directory. "No."

"She probably wouldn't let us in anyway," Rachel said.

I was thoroughly dismayed. All this planning for nothing. But just then, the door opened and two people came out. Alyssa grabbed the door before it could completely close.

We were inside, but we still didn't know the apartment number. It was Rachel who spotted the mailboxes, with names *and* numbers on them.

"Douglas, 6C," she announced.

I loved the fact that we were really working on this like a team! Three loners, united. It was a beautiful thing.

Alyssa spoke. "Okay, let's get ready."

We got our stuff out of the bag. Rachel stepped carefully into her bear costume. I put on the ears with the pink nose, and Alyssa got into the pig head. Then we stepped into the elevator. Lucky for us, it didn't stop at any other floors before reaching the sixth. No one was in the hall either when we got off, and we made it safely to the door marked with *6C*.

I imagined were both taking a deep breath, just like me. And then I knocked.

After a few seconds, we could hear footsteps. They stopped, and that was when I realized that there was a peephole in the door. My heart momentarily stopped. Who was going to open a door to kids who looked like us?

But the door *did* open. A man with grayish hair and glasses stood there. He was holding an open book in one hand, and he didn't look shocked. Just sort of puzzled.

"Is it Halloween?" he asked.

Since I was the only one with a visible face and audible voice, I spoke.

"Is Kiara home? We're friends from East Lakeside."

Now he really looked puzzled. Or maybe a little worried.

"Friends?"

I amended that. "Classmates. In the same English class."

He stepped aside and held the door open for us. "She's in her room. Down the hall, first door on the left."

The door was closed. I tapped lightly, but I didn't hear anything. So I gave the door a light push, and it opened.

I could see the back of Kiara's head. She was at her desk, focused on a computer screen, and she hadn't heard us. I coughed.

She turned and saw us, standing side by side. Her mouth opened, but nothing came out of it.

Having never heard a rabbit's voice, I did a cartoon version. "How do you do," I squealed. "I'm FunnyBunny, and we're here to ask you how you'd feel about hanging out with us sometime."

Alyssa followed. "Oink oink. I'm PigglyWiggly."

Rachel's voice was muffled, but we could just make out "BigBadBear." Then, "Thirteen." And then, "Ow!"

"What's the matter?" I asked.

"I got stuck with a pin!" She bent down to adjust her hem and I knelt to help her. In the process, my nose came off. When I got back up, Alyssa said, "Your nose is really pink now."

I touched the skin, and pink dye appeared on my finger. "Oh—oh, no!"

Then, finally, the silent Kiara spoke. Well, not exactly. She started laughing. And she kept laughing, clutching her stomach as if it hurt from the laughter. Then we were all laughing.

And I knew I'd been right about her. She was going to be one of us.

So now we are four

KIARA CAME OVER THE NEXT DAY, AND THE spyglass cooperated. When she looked through it, she saw little kids on the merry-go-round in the playground. She thought it was weird that they were playing outside with no coats on when it was so cold. But then the children's fantasies kicked in, the wooden horses became real horses, and they went galloping into the woods.

We saw several fantasies that afternoon. Rachel saw the two boys who'd teased her in English class running from a herd of elephants charging after them on Main Street. She told us that in her revenge fantasy, they were tigers, but elephants were even better. I saw Jim Berger, the skinny kid from our English class, breaking up a fight among a bunch of huge men.

Alyssa claimed that she saw me and Mike walking hand in hand, but when she let me look, I didn't see that. Personally, I think she invented it just to make me happy. But it was a fantasy I could get on board with, so I let it slide.

I actually *did* see Mike when I looked through the spyglass. He was back in the playground, pointing to a big, bright-yellow bird and jumping up and down. It was probably a once-in-a-lifetime spotting of some one-of-a-kind endangered species, and that was probably *his* fantasy.

I also saw Alyssa's. She was floating across the sky on a broomstick. She was still a witch, only this time she was all in white and looked a little like the good witch in *The Wizard of Oz*. I didn't tell her, though, and the image was gone before she looked into the spyglass again. I have a feeling it's not a fantasy she'd want to admit.

We didn't see SwanK. And I think that's a good thing.

Kiara didn't talk much, but I could tell she was

having a good time. We still don't know much about her—her family, how she got addicted to that game, why she's a loner. And we didn't ask. For now, it was enough that she wanted to be with us instead of her role-play "friends." Maybe someday we'll know more.

Meanwhile, we'll keep looking in the spyglass. We'll see fantasies, fears, and feelings. And not just ours.

Alyssa once said that nothing here in Lakeside makes sense. I still think that's true, in a way. But the spyglass put us in touch with each other. Now four confirmed loners aren't lonely anymore. For me, Lakeside has become all about making new friends. And being happy.

Makes sense to me.

The magic continues in

Rachel Takes the Lead

Read on for a sneak peek. . . .

"THIS IS A SPECIAL ANNOUNCEMENT FOR ALL seventh graders. We have two nominations for your grade representative. Submissions are closed now, and voting will take place one week from today. Your nominees are Paige Nakamura and Rachel Levin-Lopez."

Was I still daydreaming or was something wrong with my ears? A couple of classmates turned and glanced at me with surprise on their faces. Even Mr. Clark, my science teacher, was looking at me with a puzzled expression. Then I knew I'd heard correctly. My name. As a nominee for seventh-grade representative.

The bell rang, Mr. Clark dismissed us, and everyone left their desks and headed to the door. I guess I was in what they call a state of shock. My brain told me to get up but my legs wouldn't move. Finally, my limbs responded, and I rose. As I passed his desk, Mr. Clark smiled at me and said, "Congratulations, Rachel."

Congratulations? Like this was something I wanted?

There were no words to describe what I was feeling. Stunned? Upset? It was beyond all that. This has to be a mistake. Or maybe it was a joke. Someone was teasing me. But who would do something like that? There was a kid in my English class who sometimes teased me about being teacher's pet. And Paige, of course. Why would she nominate me? Because she knew she could beat me? But that didn't make any sense. If she was the only person who submitted her name, then she would have won automatically!

But when I went to my locker for my coat, Paige herself passed me in the hallway—and looked at me in such surprise that I knew it couldn't have been her.

Alyssa was waiting for me outside, and I immediately saw the shock on her face. Normally, at school, she walked around with a set expression, neither smiling nor frowning or reacting to anything at all. She always tried to look like nothing affected her one way or another. But now her mouth was open, and I had never seen her eyebrows up that high.

"What was that all about?" she asked me.

"I-I don't know!"

Then Kiara appeared. She took in our expressions and asked, "What happened?"

"Didn't you hear that announcement?" Alyssa demanded to know. "About Rachel?"

"Of course I did," Kiara replied.

"And you're not shocked?"

Kiara shook her head. "No. I already knew."

"You know who nominated me?" I asked.

Kiara nodded. "I did."